A WITCHMAS CAROL
A WICKED WITCHES OF THE MIDWEST FANTASY BOOK FOUR

AMANDA M. LEE

WINCHESTERSHAW PUBLICATIONS

Copyright © 2017 by Amanda M. Lee

All rights reserved.

No part of this book may be reproduced in any form or by any electronic or mechanical means, including information storage and retrieval systems, without written permission from the author, except for the use of brief quotations in a book review.

❦ Created with Vellum

> I've decided that Christmas is a racket. You're supposed to find the perfect gift for your perfect woman – as if anything can be that perfect – and somehow best yourself the following year. How did that even become a thing?
>
> – *Sam melting down when he can't find the perfect gift for Clove*

ONE

❄

"It's snowing."

My cousin Clove, her dark eyes sparkling, moved to the library window and looked out. It was gloomy – winters in Michigan mean darkness comes early – but I could see a hint of glittering white thanks to the outdoor landscaping lights.

"I'm glad," I said, grabbing the blanket from the back of the couch and dropping it to my lap so I could snuggle under it. "I don't like snow. It's almost Christmas, though. Who doesn't want snow for Christmas?"

My cousin Thistle, her short-cropped hair bright red with green and white accents at the tips, raised her hand as she studied a magazine. She seemed distracted, only mildly engaged in the conversation. Because we're Winchesters and believe we should always be the center of the universe that simply wouldn't do.

"Are you looking at porn or something?" I challenged.

Thistle shook her head, finally dragging her eyes to me, although it appeared she wasn't keen about expending the effort to acknowledge the fact that I was in the room with her. "If I were looking at porn, I'd be in a much better mood."

She had a point. "So … what are you looking at?"

"It's a photography magazine," Thistle replied. "Marcus got me a subscription for Christmas and the first issue showed up today. I'm going to take a photography class after the first of the year."

That sounded about right. Thistle is always interested in picking up a new skill. She's what one would call "crafty," and in more ways than one. She's a witch – we all are, for the record – so she often turns her crafty nature into something magical. She's quite talented and is opening a gallery next to her magic shop after the new year.

Me, on the other hand, I can't craft anything but an article for the weekly newspaper where I serve as editor and main reporter. The Whistler would soon be mine, though. With the help of my boyfriend, I managed to buy out my formal partner and would take ownership of Hemlock Cove's only newspaper. Okay, it's more an advertorial than a newspaper, but it would still be mine once Brian Kelly officially left town after the first of the year. That was only a week away.

Then I, Bay Winchester, would own my own business.

I was still freaking out about it.

"If you want some practice after your class, I'm always looking for freelancers to take photographs of area events," I offered. "I know it's not exactly artistic but ... ."

"No, that sounds nice." Thistle's expression was earnest. "I'd love to practice on something like that. The blurb for the class said we would start with functional photographs – which is what you would need for The Whistler – and then move on to other things."

"You sound like you're looking forward to it," Clove noted.

"I am." Thistle offered up one of her rare smiles. "I like learning new things. It's fun."

"Not me." Clove, who had recently moved in to a historical Hemlock Cove lighthouse with her fiancé Sam Cornell, wrinkled her nose. "I've been learning all sorts of things since I've been trying to cook for Sam three nights a week. Let me tell you something ... it's not fun, entertaining or educational. It's work."

I snickered, genuinely amused. Clove had been making clucking noises about how much she hated cooking for weeks now. She was a domestic soul, perfectly happy with her new reality. Cooking is something that somehow vexes us all. I think it has something to do with the fact that our mothers are all accomplished kitchen witches and can cook better while suffering from a 103-degree fever than we could on our best days. It's mildly intimidating – and altogether humbling.

"Do you want to know what I think?" Thistle asked, forgetting about her magazine and discarding it on the nearby table so she could lean closer. She spared a look for the open library door – we were at The Overlook, the inn my mother and aunts owned – and waiting for family dinner, so prying ears were genuinely a problem.

"What do you think?" Thistle has a paranoid personality. If I didn't know her better, I'd think she was stoned all the time. She's wound tighter than a reality television star's leggings, though, so I knew she wasn't dipping into Aunt Tillie's winter pot stash.

"I think that our mothers cursed us so that we can't cook."

I pursed my lips. "Why would they do that?"

"Oh, don't give me that look." Thistle extended a finger and wagged it in my face. "I know exactly what you're thinking. You think I'm living in a conspiracy theory instead of the real world. I've given this a lot of thought, though. I know it's true."

"I think you live most of your days in a conspiracy theory." I chose my words carefully because Thistle was liable to fly off the handle and attempt to make me eat dirt to shut me up. It was snowing outside, so that meant our weekly wrestling match would be conducted in the cold, and I wasn't in the mood for frozen appendages. "Still, I'm intrigued by this one. Continue."

"I hate it when you take that tone with me." Thistle wrinkled her nose, agitation evident. "You treat me as if you're the adult and I'm the child."

She wasn't wrong. Of course, two weeks ago she stole Aunt Tillie's candy cane stash and refused to return it until our elderly great-aunt promised to stop wearing bells on her house slippers. They made noise whenever she walked, driving Thistle absolutely crazy – which was, of course, Aunt Tillie's goal – so Aunt Tillie felt triumphant when

Thistle moved on her. The resulting fight wasn't exactly what I would call mature, but it was entertaining.

"Fine." I held my hands up in a placating manner. "You're completely and totally mature. If I made you feel otherwise, it was a mistake. Please continue."

Thistle made an exaggerated face. "That's not better. That's actually worse. I can hear the snark in your voice."

"If this family didn't have snark we'd have nothing to say to one another," Clove noted.

"Fine." Thistle's eyes flashed. "So, anyway, I've been thinking about the cooking thing. The witches in our family have been renowned as the best cooks in the area for generations. All three of us are terrible cooks. Why do you think that is?"

"I'm going with laziness," I answered honestly. "I tried to cook Landon breakfast the other day and he swears I gave him food poisoning. I think if we learned to do these things at an earlier age we wouldn't be struggling now."

"So you blame us?" Clove was intrigued by the suggestion. "I've been thinking of taking a cooking class after the first of the year. I want to learn to cook. I mean, even though we eat here several times a week and I don't look for that to change, I think knowing how to cook when I have my own children might come in handy."

Children? Sam and Clove were recently engaged – although they hadn't set a firm date or delved too far into their wedding preparations – but I couldn't help being surprised that the word "children" rolled so easily off her tongue.

"Screw cooking for kids," Thistle challenged. "I want to be able to cook for me."

"And Marcus," I prodded, reminding her of the boyfriend she'd officially be living within a few weeks. Technically they lived together now – in a converted barn that Marcus spent a lot of money to upgrade so they could live in it – but until the construction was complete Thistle and I shared the same roof. After that, Landon and I would be the only ones in the guesthouse. I was both looking forward to it and a little terrified. He was officially moved in (although he spent the previous night at his old apartment in Traverse City so he could clean it and hand over the keys) and we were about to embark on a new adventure.

I was so excited it made me a little nauseated. That's normal, right?

"Are you even listening to me?" Thistle chucked one of the stuffed elves Mom and my aunts placed around the house as decorations in my direction to get my attention. "I'm not joking about this theory."

"Fine." I sighed. "They cursed us so we can't cook. I believe you."

"You do not." Thistle rolled her eyes so hard I thought she might tumble out of her chair. She'd had three glasses of egg nog since we sat down, so that wasn't out of the realm of possibility. "It's true, though. None of us can cook."

"None of us can knit either," I pointed out. "They knit. Maybe they cursed us so we can't knit, too."

"I knit."

I stilled. "You do?"

Thistle bobbed her head. "Mom taught me last year. It's not hard."

I'd tried once and ended up with the most lopsided potholder ever made. That was the start – and end – of my knitting career. I shook my head to dislodge the dark thoughts I momentarily found myself swimming in. "Fine. You knit. You know what I mean, though."

"I'm more interested in what I'm talking about," Thistle said. "We can't cook even though ninety percent of our line is known for being tremendous cooks. Do you know what ninety percent of our line is also known for?"

"Being arrested?"

Thistle ignored the quip. "We're known for being selfish," she said. "I think our mothers cursed us so we can't cook so that we have no choice but to eat with them if we don't want to starve."

Under normal circumstances I would've scoffed at her theory, but the moment I tried to discard it a germ of suspicion niggled in the back of my brain. Most daughters wouldn't believe their mothers capable of anything so diabolical. I knew better.

"That's actually pretty interesting," I conceded after a few moments of quiet contemplation. "Is there a way to test this theory?"

"I don't know." Thistle rolled her neck until it cracked. "I did a little research, but then I got distracted by Christmas shopping. It's stressful to pick out the perfect Christmas gifts for the guy you're moving in with."

I wanted to scoff at the sentiment, but she wasn't wrong. "I know. Last year Landon and I had just come off a break when Christmas rolled around. We hadn't really been dating before that, so it was easy to get him something nice but impersonal for Christmas. This year is another story."

"What did you get him?" Thistle asked, intrigued.

"I'm not telling you. It's private."

"Oh, you gave in and got that bacon costume you've been teasing him with, didn't you?" Thistle adopted a knowing expression. "You're going to make Christmas a filthy holiday this year. I know it."

I didn't bother to hide my eye roll. "I'm not telling you what I got him."

"I notice you didn't deny the bacon costume," Thistle muttered.

"What did you get Marcus?" Clove asked, shifting her attention to Thistle. "This is a big holiday for you guys, too. You'd been together only a few months during Christmas last year and, if I remember correctly, you got him a book."

Thistle balked. "He loves that book."

"It was on gardening and plants," Clove said dryly. "It was a nice enough book, but it was the lamest Christmas gift ever."

Thistle's smile was sheepish. "Yeah. I kind of screwed that one up. I wasn't sure what to do. Two months is kind of early in a relationship. It seems weird now to think how nervous I was, but I kept thinking that if I went too personal with a gift that I'd be pressuring him, and that's the last thing I wanted to do."

"Well, you survived," Clove said. "Marcus is the most patient man in the world. You must've gotten him something cool this year."

"I got him quite a few things," Thistle admitted. "For one, I made a full set of dishes for the new house. They're bohemian and chic, and my pottery wheel was on fire for a few weeks. I think they're pretty cool, though."

"If Marcus were any other man I'd think that's a terrible gift." I tried to picture Landon's face if I gave him dishes. It wasn't a pretty thought. "He's the type who likes dishes, though."

"I kind of did something schmaltzy with them," Thistle offered.

The way she averted her gaze had me practically salivating. She wasn't known for being sentimental. "What?"

"Promise not to laugh?"

"That's not the Winchester way," I replied. "I promise to try not to laugh. That's the best I can do."

Thistle blew out a sigh. "Fine. You'll find out anyway, because now that Landon is living in Hemlock Cove, he and Marcus are buddies. They have their little man dates once a week. Marcus will tell Landon, and we know Landon can't keep his mouth shut and will tell you, so you'll find out anyway."

I had to snicker at Thistle's use of the term "man dates." When Landon first moved to town I worried he'd be overwhelmed by the fact that he was surrounded by females. Surprisingly, he joined a monthly poker group with Hemlock Cove's police chief Terry Davenport and started going to an area bar with Marcus one night a week without any prompting from me. I was still getting used to it.

"So, tell me," I prodded.

"I simply created a design that happens to use our initials and carved it into each dish in some fashion," Thistle replied. "I thought it was unique and ... well ... go ahead and laugh."

Strangely enough, I found I didn't want to laugh. Okay, I kind of wanted to laugh at her reaction, but the gift itself was sweet. "I think it's nice."

"Me too." Clove was sincere. "I'm not crafty the way you are. I bought Sam a bunch of stuff because he told me he wants to start fishing."

I liked Sam. No, really, it's true. It took a bit of time for me to trust him, but I recognized that he loved Clove with his whole heart, and I could never dislike him given his taste in women. Still, when I pictured Sam it wasn't ever with a fishing pole in his hand. "Are you sure he wants to fish?"

Clove shrugged. "That's what he said. I bought stuff he can return, though, because I'm not convinced. I also got him a special first edition of a Sherlock Holmes book – he loves those stories – and a big gift certificate for Home Depot because he's obsessed with getting work done on the tanker over the winter."

"That's practical and sweet," I said. "Good job."

"That leaves only you," Thistle pointed out, crossing her arms over her chest. "What did you get for Landon for Christmas?"

The question was uncomfortable enough to make me shift on the couch. "Speaking of Landon, I wonder where he is." I pushed myself to a standing position to stroll to the window and gaze out at the parking lot. "I expected him a half hour ago."

"Oh, look, she's deflecting," Thistle said. "That means she got Landon something schmaltzy, too."

"Who got Landon something schmaltzy?" Annie, the daughter of our mothers' hotel helper Belinda, popped her head into the library. She'd essentially become a member of the family in a very short period, and she loved spending time with us when we gossiped.

"Bay got Landon something schmaltzy for Christmas, but she won't tell us what it is," Thistle supplied. "You don't know, do you?"

Annie shook her head, solemn. "I don't know. What does schmaltzy mean? Is that like a code word for cool?"

"It's more a code word for emotional," Thistle replied, not missing a beat. She was often brutally honest with Annie, who looked upon Thistle with something akin to hero worship. "Bay is going to be emotional with Landon for Christmas."

"Aunt Tillie says that they're going to be naked for Christmas and it's gross," Annie said.

I narrowed my eyes. "When did Aunt Tillie tell you that?"

"Yesterday." Annie wasn't bothered by my tone. "She says you guys are up to something for Christmas. She warned Winnie, Twila and Marnie that you're going to try to pull a fast one. That's what she said; I didn't say that."

I exchanged a quick look with Thistle. While I didn't consider our Christmas plans to be anything other than ordinary, I knew very well they wouldn't leave the Winchester family matriarch happy. "Well … ."

I wasn't keen to explain things further to Annie, so I was relieved when I heard the front door of the inn open, the accompanying sound of booted feet pounding away snow assailing my ears. "That must be Landon."

I beamed as I moved past Annie, silently thankful I didn't have to delve too deep into my actual Christmas plans, and grinned when I found my boyfriend standing in the decked-out lobby. "I was getting worried."

Landon's smile was soft as he glanced in my direction. "Do you really think I'd miss our first Christmas living together?"

"No. Not for a second. That doesn't mean I wasn't worried about you being on the road."

"The roads aren't terrible yet." Landon held out his hand for me to join him. "They're going to get that way in a few hours, though. By then we'll be locked in the guesthouse with absolutely nobody bothering us for forty-eight hours straight."

That sounded positively heavenly. "I ran to the store so we can officially be hermits without worrying about starving."

"Good deal." Landon pressed a kiss to my mouth. "I think it's going to be a pretty good Christmas. You. Me. Wine. What more could we want?"

As if on cue, Aunt Tillie appeared in the door. The expression on her face told me her radar was up and she was about to go on a rampage.

"What's going on?" I asked, shifting nervously.

Aunt Tillie didn't crack a smile, instead extending a finger and letting loose with a hissing sound. "You're all on my list."

And here we go.

> I hate when women say they don't want anything for Christmas … or Valentine's Day … or birthdays. They always say that, but you know it's not true. Bay is a beautiful woman, but if I show up Christmas morning without a gift she'll turn into the Hulk and smash me.

— *Landon on Christmas gifts*

TWO

❄

"Merry Christmas, Aunt Tillie."

Landon took me by surprise when he greeted my curmudgeonly great-aunt with a bright smile.

Aunt Tillie anticipated a set-up, her lip curling. She's often evil, so she can sense when others are about to do something she won't like – it's a gift we wish she'd return for store credit – and the look she scorched Landon with was right out of a horror movie.

"It's not Christmas yet," Aunt Tillie pointed out. "It's Christmas Eve. Tomorrow is Christmas."

"I think the sentiment is for the entire holiday season, not just one day." Landon shrugged out of his coat and placed it on the ornate coatrack in the corner. "You don't seem as if you're in the Christmas spirit. Is something wrong?"

"Oh, I know what you're doing." Aunt Tillie extended a gnarled finger. "Don't think for a second that I don't know what you're doing."

Since being introduced to the Winchester witches fourteen months ago, Landon had become accustomed to our peculiar ways. Sometimes he found Aunt Tillie's antics amusing, other times frustrating. He appeared to be in such a good mood today that nothing she said could bother him.

"I'm fine with that." Landon slipped his arm around my waist and slid me a sidelong look. "The apartment is completely empty. I have two more boxes of stuff in the Explorer, but I turned over the keys and you're officially stuck with me."

"It's a tough job, but I think I'll survive."

"I think so, too." Landon tugged me toward the library, paying very little attention to Aunt Tillie. That would only serve to infuriate her more, something Landon knew well, but he didn't seem bothered by the potential mayhem flitting across her face.

He released me when he caught sight of Annie in the library, scooping her off her feet and tickling her until she gasped from raucous giggles. "Look what I found, Bay." He beamed at the girl as her face grew red. "I think I found one of Santa's elves."

"I'm not an elf," Annie sputtered, struggling against Landon's ministrations as he sat on the couch. "Elves aren't real."

"Who told you that?" Thistle asked, arching an eyebrow. "I happen to know for a fact that elves are real."

Annie was at that age when questioning the existence of Santa Claus was normal. This year, despite comments to the contrary, she was hedging her bets because she didn't want to miss out on gifts. Next year she would probably be over the whole Santa thing, but part of the magic remained this year.

"Have you really seen elves?"

It took me a moment to realize Annie was talking to me. I tilted my head to the side as I reclaimed the blanket and got comfortable on the couch. "I haven't seen them, but I've heard them."

"I've seen them," Thistle said. "Santa makes two ride in his sleigh with him so he can streamline his gift-giving process. True story."

Annie looked dubious. "Really?"

Thistle nodded. "Really. The elves are Santa's special helpers. They do most of the work while he gets all the glory."

Landon made a face. "Don't tell her that."

Annie seemed intrigued by Thistle's explanation. "Kind of like you guys and Aunt Tillie when you solve a murder, huh?"

Hmm. That was an interesting observation. "Exactly like that."

"Wait a second ... ." Landon shifted so Annie was upright and he could look at me. "Don't I usually help when it comes to solving murders?"

"Yes," Thistle answered without hesitation. "I don't know how we'd get through each case without you pointing at Bay and saying, 'You're in really big trouble.'"

Annie giggled hysterically at Thistle's impersonation of Landon. "She sounded just like you."

Landon rolled his eyes. "She did not. That's hardly the point, though. Everyone helps solve murders in this house."

"Except I do all the heavy lifting," Aunt Tillie volunteered as she strolled into the room. Her gaze bounced between faces, something worrisome flitting across her features. "I'm Santa and they're elves. You got that exactly right, Annie."

If Annie worshipped Thistle, she downright adored Aunt Tillie. She thought there was nothing the elderly witch could do wrong. "What time do you think Santa will come tonight?"

"When you're asleep," Landon replied, poking her side. "He knows when you're sleeping, so he'll wait until he's sure you're out."

"That's kind of unfair," Annie said, jutting out her lower lip. "I'd feel better about him being real if I could see him."

"You have to take it on faith," Landon said. "You've been a good girl this year. I'm sure you'll get your fair share of gifts."

"I'm sure you'll get more than your fair share," Aunt Tillie corrected. "I talked to Santa, and he said you're getting extra this year."

Landon shifted his gaze to Aunt Tillie. "I'm not sure you should tell her that."

"And I'm not sure I care what you think," Aunt Tillie challenged. "Annie has been good. She'll be rewarded because of that."

Annie's eyes sparkled under the compliment. "I sure hope so. You guys are coming for breakfast, right? You'll be here for Christmas, won't you?"

The question caught me off guard. I expected it to become an issue after dinner, when my mother asked what time we would be arriving for breakfast. I hadn't yet told her that we planned to be hermits in the guesthouse and spend our first real Christmas together, away from them, just the two of us.

Clove and Thistle planned the same with their respective love interests. We'd talked about it at length, agreed to approach our mothers as a unit, and then proceeded to put it off for as long as humanly possible. We were officially out of time, and the fallout was bound to be uncomfortable for everyone.

"We'll be here the day after Christmas," Landon replied, his smile firmly in place. "We're going to spend Christmas Day alone at the guesthouse."

Annie didn't look happy with the announcement. "But ... why?"

"Because it's our first real Christmas together," Landon explained. "It's a big deal for us, especially since we just moved in together. We want to spend some quiet time alone with one another."

"But ... why?"

"Because ... ." Landon broke off and spared me a glance. "Do you want to help me here?"

"I think you're doing fine." I slid a worried look in Aunt Tillie's direction and found her glowering. "It's not a big deal."

"It's a very big deal," Aunt Tillie argued. "Why do you think you're all on my list?"

Hmm. That was interesting. "Did you already know?"

"I heard your mothers talking," Aunt Tillie replied. "Apparently Terry told them what you had planned. They're all very upset. In fact, they're in the kitchen right now ... crying."

"Terry, huh?" I glared at Landon. "Did you tell Chief Terry what we were planning?"

"I didn't realize it was a big deal," Landon argued. "I'm still not sure why it's a big deal. Would you like to share with the class what I'm missing?"

"Christmas is a day for family," Aunt Tillie barked. "We're supposed to spend it together as a family. We're not supposed to break apart into small little factions and do ... well, whatever dirty things the six of you have planned."

"I have nothing dirty planned," Landon said. "It's not about that. We simply want to spend a whole day together, just the two of us, in front of a fire. I'm not sure why you're melting down here."

Aunt Tillie snorted. "I'm hardly melting down."

"It doesn't look that way to me."

I risked a glance in Thistle's direction and found her watching the scene with a mixture of curiosity and amusement. Oddly enough, while informing our mothers of our plans was worrisome, it was telling Aunt Tillie that filled us with dread. The only time she believed in total family unity was Christmas. It was her favorite time of year. We expected a negative reaction, but this one looked as if it would spiral downward in terrific fashion before we could gain control of the conversation.

"Aunt Tillie, we're spending tonight together. That's the same as spending Christmas Day together." I swallowed hard. "It'll be okay."

"Oh, it's not going to be okay." Aunt Tillie's expression was dark. "It's going to be pretty far from okay." She straightened her shoulders and landed a weighted look on each of us. "You'll be sorry you decided to spend Christmas away from me. I can promise you that."

"We're spending tonight with you," Landon argued. "That's spending Christmas with you."

"Whatever." Aunt Tillie usually spends more time threatening us with final words before storming out of a room. This time she merely swept out without a backward glance. It was beyond worrisome.

"You hurt her feelings," Annie snapped, fighting her way clear of Landon and glaring as she stomped across the room. Apparently she was picking up Aunt Tillie's dramatic slack this evening. "You should be nicer to her."

"We're not trying to be mean to her, Annie," Thistle said. "We just want a quiet Christmas. I'm pretty sure that's allowed."

"I'm pretty sure you were mean to Aunt Tillie, and I don't like you now." Annie stalked out of the room, refusing to look in our direction as she exited.

"Well, that was … delightful," Clove muttered.

"She'll be fine," Thistle said. "It's honestly not a big deal. She won't even remember why she was angry tomorrow morning."

"I'm sure." I said the words, but I wasn't sure I believed them. "We should head to dinner. We'll have to explain things to our mothers before Aunt Tillie bends their ears."

"Oh, well, I'm totally looking forward to that." Thistle made a face. "They'll be fine."

I wanted to believe her, but I wasn't so sure. Still, Landon was looking forward to a quiet day. I had no intention of going back on my word and taking it from him.

"They'll definitely be fine."

I could only hope I was right.

"WELL, THAT WAS THE MOST uncomfortable dinner ever."

Landon carried a large moving box into the guesthouse living room and rested it on the floor before yanking off his boots and coat. He gave the box a wide berth as he threw himself on the couch and let loose a dramatic sigh.

"I'm glad there weren't a bunch of guests at the inn," I admitted, putting away my own coat and boots before sinking to the floor next to the box. It was automatic for me. We'd spent weeks finding a place for all of Landon's belongings. I wanted him to feel as if this was his home, which meant getting rid of every box. "If we had guests, I think they would've been asking for refunds."

"Did Aunt Tillie say one word during dinner?"

"She said a few words," I replied. "Almost all of them were curse words, though, and she mumbled them under her breath so Annie wouldn't hear."

"Yes, well, Annie was a problem all her own. I've never seen her so despondent."

"Yeah. I don't know what to make of that."

I was lost in my own little world, my mind busy with images of dinner playing through it. Mom kept a stiff upper lip when I informed her of our plans, wishing us well before focusing on dinner. She put on a brave front, but I could tell she was bothered.

"What is all this stuff?" I asked, turning my attention to the box.

Landon grinned. "That is my remembrance box."

I arched an eyebrow, amused despite myself. "Your remembrance box?"

"Yup."

"I thought that was a girl thing."

"Mock all you want, but that is a box of memories from my childhood, my high school years ... maybe a little bit of college stuff made it in. All my work awards are in there. I have a bunch of stuff that reminds me of you in there."

Ah, now we were getting somewhere. "You have stuff that reminds you of me?" I was excited at the prospect. "What stuff?"

"Go ahead and look." Landon remained on the couch, his eyes contemplative as I tore through the box.

The first memento I stumbled across was a photograph of Landon and his brothers. They were young, but I recognized Landon and his vivid blue eyes right away. "When was this?"

Landon looked over my shoulder. "Christmas. I think I was eight. We got a train set, which we didn't ask for. My father always wanted a train set, so he bought one for us. We weren't excited at first, but we grew to love the stupid thing because our father loved it so much."

"You were cute." I ran my index finger over the photograph. "It's weird, but I feel as if I'd recognize you no matter the time now."

"I feel like I'd recognize you, too."

"Are you upset because we're not with your family for Christmas?"

Landon immediately started shaking his head. "No. I'm exactly where I want to be. We're going to do what I want, which is nothing but hang out together and enjoy a full day in our pajamas. I want a fire, food and you."

"That sounds nice." I returned my attention to the box, my stomach flipping when I caught a glance of something I recognized. "What's this?"

Landon moved to the floor so he'd have an easier time watching me go through his memories. He grinned when I held up a box with a handful of dried flowers in it.

"What do you think it is?"

"I ... ." I broke off, chewing my bottom lip. I had an inkling. I recognized the flowers. If I was right, that would mean Landon was even more sentimental than I realized. "They look like the flowers I brought you in the hospital after you got shot protecting us."

"They are."

"Really?" My heart did a happy dance, which made me feel ridiculous. It was Christmas, though. If you can't be schmaltzy on Christmas, when can you?

"I kept some of them, although even now I have no idea why." Landon rubbed his hand over my back. "I didn't want to throw them out. I can't explain why or what possessed me to put them in the box. I even bought a special box from one of those craft stores just to store the flowers."

I smirked. "That's kind of cute."

"Other people would call it being whipped."

"You say that like it's a bad thing."

Landon poked my side. "It's not a bad thing." He wrapped his arm around my waist and tugged me away from the box, settling me so I was pressed snugly against him and resting his head on my shoulder. "If you want to go to the inn tomorrow, we can."

"It's supposed to practically be a blizzard tonight."

"Yes, and Aunt Tillie has a plow," Landon reminded me. "She could pick us up."

"You hate riding with her when she's using her plow."

Landon's lips curved. "When I came back after ... well, you know what after. When I came back after deciding that I didn't care you were a witch and I wanted you no matter what, one of the first things I saw was Aunt Tillie plowing. I remember thinking 'and you want to voluntarily spend time with these crazy people.' I was convinced I was losing it."

"And yet you stayed."

"I stayed and I never want to leave." Landon pressed a kiss to my neck. "Aunt Tillie was weird about us wanting to stay here instead of going to the inn tomorrow morning. Why?"

"Christmas is her favorite time of year," I replied. "She's generally not one for spending too much time with family ... except for Christmas."

"Why do you think that is?"

I shrugged. "I don't know. She's never really talked about it all that much. She spent a lot of time with us during the Christmas season when we were kids."

"Really? I was under the impression she hated spending time with you girls because she wasn't fond of babysitting."

"She always says things like that but they're not really true." I was rueful. "She liked spending time with us. She used to take us plowing with her. We would bury the end of Mrs. Little's driveway with snow – and then sometimes use magic to turn it yellow – and she would take us to the bakery for doughnuts and hot chocolate when we were done terrorizing her enemies."

"That sounds fun."

"When you're eight that type of stuff is always fun. Heck, it was still fun when we were sixteen."

Landon chuckled. "We can go there tomorrow and spend a few hours with your family. I'm perfectly fine with that. I know you agreed to spend the day with me because I made that comment about spending the perfect day together. We can adjust our plans."

"Then it wouldn't be the perfect day."

"There is no such thing as perfect, sweetie," Landon argued. "As long as I'm with you, I don't care what we do."

It was a nice sentiment, but I wasn't sure I believed him. "We'll play it by ear," I said, opting to compromise. "If we feel guilty tomorrow morning, we'll head to the inn."

"That sounds like a plan." Landon pulled me closer. "Until then, though, I thought we might play a game."

I relaxed a bit at his teasing tone. "Oh, yeah? What kind of game?"

"How do you feel about making snow angels?"

"That sounds cold."

"Naked snow angels."

"That sounds even colder."

"I thought we could cheat and make them in the bathtub."

I snickered as he tickled my side, laughing as I melted against him. "That sounds like the perfect way to spend an evening."

"I thought so."

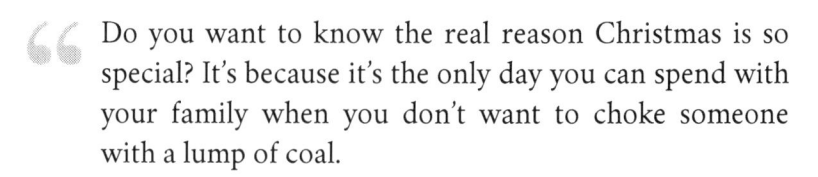

" Do you want to know the real reason Christmas is so special? It's because it's the only day you can spend with your family when you don't want to choke someone with a lump of coal.

— *Aunt Tillie feeling nostalgic in front of the Christmas tree*

THREE

*L*andon's body was warm against mine when I woke the next morning, the sound of the snow blowing outside serving to lull me into a comfort coma. I considered falling back asleep. It was right there, after all. I could drift right back under. I didn't feel completely rested.

Instead I opened my eyes, hoping to get a brief glimpse through the window. I heard the wind whistling past the entire night and knew we were due for a big snow when we finally braved the day. Instead of looking at the window, I found myself staring at a blank wall.

I blinked several times in rapid succession, my morning-muddled mind struggling to find something to hold onto. Even after thirty seconds of hard staring, my eyes traveling over a room I barely recognized, I knew that something was very wrong.

I slid away from Landon, just far enough so I could turn my head and study his features. Part of me worried I'd wake up next to someone else – not because I was known for hopping into bed with others, but rather because I'd been cursed into a few odd scenarios that involved me opening my eyes and finding myself in strange

AMANDA M. LEE

places. Once I woke in a fairy tale world, in a bed owned by bears. No joke.

I couldn't hide my relieved sigh when Landon's familiar face met my gaze.

"It's early," Landon murmured, never opening his eyes. "Go back to sleep."

"Um ... ." I didn't know what to say. Blurting out, "We're in someone else's house" seemed the wrong way to go. Still, he needed to know. Of course, there was always the possibility this was a dream. That would be a nice change of pace given our last few mishaps.

I pressed my eyes shut, sucked in a cleansing breath and prayed for sleep. If I could fall asleep, surely I would wake up in my own bed. After a few minutes of trying to force my mind to return to slumber I gave up and stared at the ceiling. There was something familiar about the room, something I couldn't quite identify from my position. That didn't mean I was happy about our predicament.

"Landon?"

"Sleep, sweetie." Landon brushed a distracted kiss against my ear. "It's Christmas. We can sleep as long as we want."

That sounded nice. Of course, it only sounded nice when I pictured doing it in my own bed.

"Landon." There was more urgency in my tone this time. "Open your eyes."

"You're beautiful regardless, Bay," Landon said. "I'm fine if you have bedhead all day."

That was something of a sore spot for me – I can never understand how he wakes up looking better than when he went to bed but I look as if a windstorm crashed through my hair – but now was not the time to focus on that.

"Thank you for the compliment. I love hearing it."

"Good. You're my pretty girl."

"That makes me sound like a dog."

"Ruff." Landon made mock growling noises as he snuggled closer. He still hadn't opened his eyes.

I didn't want to ruin the day for him. He told me weeks before, in a moment of weakness, about these big plans he had for us to do nothing but enjoy each other on Christmas Day. At the time it sounded romantic. Now, though, we had another issue scratching at the door.

"Landon."

"Bay, if you want me to give you a present early I need to wake up."

It took me a moment to realize what he meant. "Oh, geez." My stomach twisted. "Now is so not the time for a rousing game of naked monkeys jumping on the bed."

Landon snickered. "I've never really thought of it that way, but I'm always in the mood for naked monkeys ... or morning cuddles." As if to prove his point, he tightened his grip on me. "Now ... go back to sleep. I just need fifteen more minutes."

"Really? Do you think fifteen minutes is going to make this situation better?"

"What situation?"

Here was the opening I was looking for. "We're not in our bed."

"Oh, yeah? Where are we?" Landon sounded distracted, his hands busy as he rubbed them over my midriff.

"Someone else's bed."

"Are you playing a game? Are we in Santa's bed?"

"More like some random person's bed."

"Oh, well ... ." Landon finally wrenched open his eyes, his smile lazy until he took in the room. He bolted to a sitting position, letting loose with a string of curse words that would've put him on Santa's naughty list in a heartbeat. "What the ... ?"

"Good morning, sunshine," I drawled. "Welcome to another titillating round of 'Where am I now?'"

Landon's mouth dropped open as he surveyed the room, frustration evident as it positively dripped from his pores. "Where are we?"

"I have no idea, but there is something vaguely familiar about this room. I can't quite put my finger on it."

Landon narrowed his eyes. "Are you saying we're in some former boyfriend's room?"

That hadn't even occurred to me. "Oh, well ... ."

"If some guy you used to date wanders in here, I'm not joking, I'm totally going to start throwing punches."

I tilted my head to the side as I pulled myself up, giving the room a more thorough scan. "I don't think I ever dated anyone who slept in a room like this."

"Strangely enough, that doesn't make me feel better." Landon tossed off the covers and hopped to his feet, coming to a complete halt when he stared down at his pajamas. "What is this?"

I hissed out a sound halfway between a chuckle and a gasp as I studied his flannel pajamas. They were straight out of some Lifetime Christmas movie – red and green slashing patterns with happy snowmen decorating the fabric. "You look kind of cute," I hedged.

"I look like an idiot," Landon countered. "I look like … ."

"You're really happy it's Christmas," I finished, sliding out of the bed and frowning at my own pajamas. They matched Landon's almost exactly, except mine were adorned with mistletoe and odd little angels with demonic smiles on their faces. "I think I'm going to be sick."

"Oh, it's not so funny now, is it?" Landon scowled as he worked his way around the bed, glaring at the oak headboard. "This bed looks old."

"It's an antique."

"Do you think we're traveling through time again?"

That was an interesting question and it had crossed my mind at least twice since I woke. Several months before, Aunt Tillie drew us into her memories when she was unconscious following an accident. Despite being agitated, Landon declared – once we were safely back in our time, of course – that he'd enjoyed the trip. Now, faced with another, he didn't seem so certain.

"I don't know." I moved to the closed door across the way and tested the handle. It turned without incident.

"Did you think we were locked in here?" Landon asked.

"I was just checking."

"You'd better hope this isn't some ex-boyfriend's house," Landon muttered. "I can just see Aunt Tillie punishing us by bringing back every guy you used to love and throwing them in my face."

"I don't think you have to worry about that. You're the only guy I've ever loved."

Landon pursed his lips. "I wasn't fishing ... ."

"You still caught the big one, though, right?" I teased.

Landon's chuckle caused me to settle a bit. The weird angels on my pajamas seemed to be staring, which made me uncomfortable, but the laughter relieved the ball of tension building in my stomach.

"I needed that." Landon rested his hand on my shoulder before reaching around me with his free hand. "Should we see what fresh hell Aunt Tillie has unleashed upon us this time?"

"I think it's funny that we both automatically assume Aunt Tillie did this to us," I noted. "It could be a dream ... or an evil curse from some other demented witch."

"We both know it's Aunt Tillie." Landon kept his body close to mine as he pushed open the door, his muscles taut and ready for action should something jump out. Wherever we were, the house remained calm and quiet. "Hmm."

Landon poked his head into the hallway, keeping a protective arm out to make sure I stayed behind him in case something horrible hopped out to eat us. When it didn't happen, he dropped the arm and I moved up beside him.

"Maybe we're trapped in an empty house because she wants to teach us a lesson about abandoning family around the holidays," Landon suggested.

"She's definitely trying to teach us a lesson." I moved, flicking my eyes to a large painting on the hallway wall. "I don't think we're going to end up alone, though."

"Why is that?" Landon followed me, his eyes moving to the painting. His mouth dropped open when he realized we were looking at a bright landscape with a multitude of dancing witch silhouettes highlighting the wooded atmosphere. "I've seen this before."

"You have," I confirmed, bobbing my head. "It's in Aunt Tillie's bedroom."

"So we're in a Winchester house?" Landon rolled his shoulders as he swiveled to look back the way we came. "Wait a second ... ." He recognized the hallway from our previous stroll down Winchester memory lane. "This is the old house you used to live in."

"It's technically the same house," I clarified. "It's just gone through multiple renovations since this time period."

"And when is this time period?"

I shrugged. "I'm not sure, but ... ." I cast a glance back to the bedroom we vacated. "I'm pretty sure that's the room I was born in."

That was another memory from Aunt Tillie's mad trip to the past. Not many people can say they witnessed their own birth. I did, though. Landon was with me. He was gobsmacked and utterly charmed by the event. I was mostly grossed out because I was forced to look at my mother's lady parts.

"That is where you were born," Landon confirmed, lacing his fingers with mine as he tugged me along the hallway. "That means the staircase is this way."

I had no idea why he was so excited to find the staircase. Descending to the main floor wouldn't solve our predicament. If I knew Aunt Tillie – and I understood the way her mind worked better than most – there was no way we could climb out of this situation until she showed us exactly what she wanted us to see. And because she idles at difficult, she'd show us in the most annoying way possible.

Landon was quiet as he led me down the stairs, his eyes keen when we hit the first floor. The entire place was decked out in Christmas decorations, although they weren't the same ones I remembered from my childhood. These decorations were older, a little more worn around the edges. Still, I remembered a few pieces from my childhood.

"Do you see that?" I stopped in front of the Christmas tree and pointed toward the fragile-looking star on the top.

Landon remained close. "Yeah."

"That was my grandmother's star."

"Do you think she's still alive in this memory?"

"Not necessarily. The star was around for a long time after she was gone."

"I didn't see it on the tree this year."

"That's because it was broken when we were kids," I replied. "It was the first Christmas we shared under this roof after we all moved in together. Thistle and I were messing around and we accidentally broke it."

"Did you get in trouble?"

"I expected to. We hid what we did at first, but Aunt Tillie had a meltdown when she couldn't find the star, and eventually we had to own up to what we did."

Landon understood the sentiment tugging at my heart. "I know she loved your grandmother very much. It must've upset her to lose an important piece of your grandmother like that."

"She wasn't angry as much as she was upset," I replied, racking my memory for a picture of the day it happened. "She disappeared into her room for a long time. We thought she might kick us out of the house because of what we did – Thistle was all for that because they fought like crazy even then – but when Aunt Tillie returned she was fine."

"That doesn't sound like her at all. She usually likes to teach you girls a lesson."

"She does, but she said something that day that I kind of forgot about until just now," I said, rubbing my finger over my lip. "She said the holidays weren't about things, but feelings. While she would miss the star, she said that she knew Grandma Ginger would be happy that it died a good death.

"I didn't understand what she meant by that," I continued. "Then she said that Grandma always wanted us to grow up in the big house, so she would've been happy to sacrifice the star as long as it meant we were together as a family."

"Ah." Realization dawned on Landon's face. "Even though you said it multiple times, it's just starting to sink in. I'm getting the feeling that Christmas is important to Aunt Tillie."

"It always has been."

"Which means she'll punish us for wanting to be alone," Landon mused, turning so he could look around the room. "It doesn't look as if you guys are living here yet. There aren't any toys lying around and there's only one stocking hanging over the fireplace."

I followed his gaze, smiling when I saw the over-sized stocking hanging alone. It was big enough to fit a giant and "Tillie" was emblazoned across the top.

"She had that stocking for years," I supplied. "She had ones made for Thistle, Clove and me, too. My mother had a fit because she thought they were overbearing, but now I think she likes them."

"I've seen the stockings," Landon noted. "I also saw that someone put stockings up for Marcus, Sam and me this year. That was a nice touch. Your mother?"

"Aunt Tillie."

Landon stilled. "Seriously? I didn't think she liked me that much."

"She loves you even when she hates you. As for the stockings, that's simply part of Christmas." I felt a bit misty admitting it. "She really does love Christmas."

Landon slid a sidelong gaze to me. "I'm starting to think you do, too."

I shook myself out of my self-serving reverie. "I love Christmas. Halloween is still my favorite."

"Yeah, but you're feeling guilty about agreeing to have a private Christmas party for just the two of us."

I balked. "No."

Landon arched a challenging eyebrow.

"Okay, maybe a little bit," I hedged. "It's just … I can't really remember Christmases before Aunt Tillie. That first one in this house – the Christmas right after our fathers left and Aunt Tillie took us in – was this black hole of depression until she stepped up and gave us a Christmas we could never forget."

"Was that the one where you got the dog?"

"Sugar. She was a good dog. I cried for days when she died. So did Aunt Tillie."

"Bay, you should've told me that you wanted to spend Christmas with your family," Landon said. "I thought you wanted to spend it with me."

"I do want to spend it with you."

Landon held his hands up. "I know you want to spend it with me. I didn't mean it the way it came out. But you want to spend it with them, too."

He wasn't wrong, but still .... "I'm not sure I realized that I wanted to spend it with them until right now. I was all for the alone time when I suggested it, but now I realize it was a bit selfish."

"And I think you believed you would be ruining the Christmas holiday for me if you said anything," Landon countered. "It's okay. I love your family almost as much as I love you. I have no problem spending Christmas with them."

"Really?"

"Of course. Jeez." Landon pulled me to him for a hug. "You're so much work, woman."

"I know. I don't mean to be."

"I think you do, but there's absolutely nothing to fight about." He pressed a kiss to my forehead. "Aunt Tillie has already made her point. We can wake up from this nightmare before it really gets started. I think that's progress, don't you? It took us forever to work our way through the fairy tale world ... and hours to work through Aunt Tillie's memories. We worked through this one in ten minutes. We should get an award."

I chuckled at the way he puffed out his chest. "Hopefully this will all fall away really soon."

"You'd like that, wouldn't you?"

I recognized Aunt Tillie's voice right away and spun around, widening my eyes when I saw her standing on the staircase. She was dressed in an elf costume – complete with curled-toe shoes – and her smile was serene.

"We get it," I said, mustering a smile. "We'll be there for Christmas breakfast."

"Bright and early," Landon added. "We're looking forward to it."

"You can send us home now," I said hopefully.

"Oh, so sweet and cute." Aunt Tillie beamed, her smile lighting up her face. Then she shifted and the corners of her mouth fell. "Now pull your heads out of your behinds, because nothing is that easy. You're just getting started, kids."

Landon groaned. "I just knew it wouldn't be that easy."

Aunt Tillie sarcastically mock applauded. "Hey, you're smarter than you look. Of course, that would have to be a given, wouldn't it?"

"Oh, man." Landon slapped his hand to his forehead. "Here we go again."

> Christmas is my favorite time of year because it's all about family. Actually, that's what normal people say about the holidays. We're talking about people who don't have to live in this family. Christmas is still my favorite time of year, don't get me wrong, but there are times I could take or leave my family.

—Winnie when Thistle starts complaining about this year's choice of Christmas cookies

FOUR

"What's your angle?"

Landon crossed his arms over his chest, doing his best to look tough. He was still dressed in the worst Christmas pajamas ever, so his "bad boy" attitude lost a bit in translation. I didn't bother pointing that out.

"What makes you think I have an angle?" Aunt Tillie adopted the innocent expression she reserved for when the Michigan State Police showed up on our doorstep once a year to question her about rumors regarding an alleged pot field on our property.

"Because you always have an angle," Landon replied. "We just told you that we've learned our lesson. We want to be with the family for Christmas. Despite this ... whatever it is ... that includes you. We don't need to be manipulated further."

"I don't manipulate people."

Landon and I snorted in unison.

"I don't," Aunt Tillie pressed. "I'm a live-and-let-live sort of person. Manipulation is beneath me."

"Since when?" I challenged.

"Since forever. Apparently you don't remember what Christmas was like before me, before I graced you with my benevolent light. I clearly need to remind you."

Landon craned his neck, making a big show of looking around the room.

"What are you doing?" I asked.

"Looking for the television cameras," Landon replied. "We're very clearly being set up for a bad reality show."

"Oh, puh-leez." Aunt Tillie rolled her eyes. "If I wanted to embarrass you I wouldn't need a camera."

Sadly, I knew she was right. Still, Christmas was Aunt Tillie's favorite time of year. You could never describe the woman as a giant marshmallow – or even the frayed end of a Q-tip – but she softened around the holiday season. She couldn't seem to help herself. I wanted to take advantage of that.

"We're really sorry." I kept my tone light and even. "We didn't realize how much we'd miss by cutting ourselves off for Christmas. You have to know that we weren't doing it out of malice. We just wanted a ... magical day."

"Oh, you're going to get one." Aunt Tillie smiled as the grandfather clock in the corner chimed. "You two should really get ready. It's almost time for dinner."

I knit my eyebrows, confused. "It's morning. We just woke up."

"No, it's noon." Aunt Tillie pointed at the clock for emphasis.

She was right. Both hands rested on the twelve. "Is this a dream?"

"I don't deal in dreams."

"No, but you're not above manipulating them."

"I just told you that I don't manipulate people!" Aunt Tillie's eyes flashed with annoyance. "Are you purposely trying to irritate me?"

"Not really, but I am curious why we're the only ones here," I admitted. "Why aren't Clove and Thistle here? They made plans to stay at home Christmas Day, too."

"Don't you worry about what Clove and Thistle are doing," Aunt Tillie ordered. "They're having their own adventures."

"Like we are?"

"Let's just say I tailored something special for both of them and leave it at that," Aunt Tillie suggested. "Their transgressions were different from yours."

"Transgressions?" My eyebrows flew up my forehead. "What transgressions? We made a mistake. We told you that we're sorry. We've learned the lesson you wanted us to learn. Why can't we be done?"

"Because this was never about learning a lesson."

"Then what was it about?"

"Punishment." Aunt Tillie's smile was smug. "You need to learn what happens when you hurt my feelings."

"Oh, geez. I don't like the sound of this." Landon pinched the bridge of his nose and stared at the ceiling. "Can't you just curse Bay to smell like bacon and punish her that way? That's a very effective punishment."

"That's a reward for you," Aunt Tillie countered. "I blame you for this situation, so there's no way I'm going to reward you."

"I didn't know Christmas was such a big deal for you," Landon argued. "I wasn't trying to be difficult. Heck, I wasn't trying to be mean. Believe it or not, the last thing I want to do is hurt your feelings."

"I don't believe it." Aunt Tillie was obstinate on a good day. Apparently today she was bound and determined to set a record for ticket prices on the stubborn subway.

Landon opened his mouth to respond, but I rested my hand on his arm to still him. Arguing would only force her to dig her heels in. We needed to approach her in a different manner. "What do you want us to do?"

"Participate."

"In what? Dinner?"

Aunt Tillie nodded. "It won't be just dinner, of course. But it's a nice start."

"Okay, fine. We'll have dinner with you."

"Great." Aunt Tillie's smile was back in place. "You'll need to change first."

"Why? Is someone else coming to dinner?"

Aunt Tillie nodded. "Numerous other people."

"Okay, well ... we have nothing to change into."

"I'll fix that." Aunt Tillie's eyes gleamed as she snapped her fingers. Miraculously, Landon and I found ourselves wearing different outfits. They were even more hideous than the garish pajamas we wore mere seconds before.

"Oh, man." Landon tugged on his ugly Christmas sweater. It was easy because Rudolph's head was huge and the nose, which was dead center on his chest, actually protruded in a little nubbin. "Are you trying to make me suffer?"

"I just consider it an added bonus," Aunt Tillie replied. She'd changed, too, although her outfit was much nicer. She wore a burgundy dress and a set of pearls I knew Uncle Calvin – her late husband – had bought her.

"Why do you get to look nice and we look like morons?" I asked, glaring at the ugly cardigan she forced on me. It was bright red and boasted a herd of frolicking cats. I hate the color red, although I have no idea why. As for the cats? They looked a bit demented, possibly possessed, and keen to take over the world when they thought no one was looking.

"Perhaps it's part of your punishment," Aunt Tillie suggested, clapping her hands when the doorbell rang. "Our guests are here."

I watched her scamper across the room, my emotions vacillating wildly. "Who is here?"

"You are."

"Me?"

"And your mother and father."

My stomach jolted at the words. "This is a Christmas memory from before my dad left?" I couldn't help being intrigued. "That must be why I don't remember it."

"What happens when they see us?" Landon asked. "I mean ... will they be able to see us? Last time we were trapped in your memory certain people could see us and others couldn't. Will it be like that?"

"No, because you're not trapped in my memory." Aunt Tillie stopped in front of a mirror to check her reflection. "This is real."

She said the words, but her magical clothes-changing trick seemed to indicate otherwise. "This doesn't feel real."

"Give it time." Aunt Tillie plastered a wide smile on her face before pulling open the door. "Merry Christmas!"

The couple standing on the other side of the door looked anything but merry. In fact, Mom and Dad looked downright miserable. Despite that fact, Mom greeted Aunt Tillie with a wide hug while Dad slid around her and led a younger version of me inside.

"Look at you." Landon smiled at the little girl in the bright Christmas dress. She had bouncing blonde curls and black dress shoes. "How cute were you?"

I didn't particularly find the outfit cute. The solemn look on my face was even less cute. "I don't remember this," I murmured.

"Well, then it will be fun for both of us," Landon said. "It might be an entertaining diversion."

"That's not what you said a few minutes ago," I reminded him.

"Yes, well, these side jaunts Aunt Tillie keeps sending us on make me feel as if I'm on an emotional rollercoaster. I can't always help it."

I didn't blame him.

"We're a little early, but I brought pies," Mom said, drawing my attention to her and Aunt Tillie. "We're so excited to spend Christmas with you."

"I'll bet." Aunt Tillie's smile slipped as she focused on Dad. "And how are you, Jack?"

"Thrilled with life," Dad deadpanned, releasing little Bay's hand as he reached for the television remote. "Can't you tell?"

"Jack." Mom's voice was full of warning. "We talked about this. We're not doing this in front of Bay."

I pursed my lips as I focused on the little girl, who very clearly didn't miss the harsh exchange. "They always said that. They weren't going to fight in front of me, but they always did. They didn't realize that fighting about fighting was still fighting."

"It must be hard for you," Landon noted. "You said you don't really remember Christmases before you moved in with Aunt Tillie. This doesn't seem like a happy one."

"That's not entirely true," I hedged. "I remembered bits and pieces. I don't remember this particular moment, but I remember a few things from my last Christmas with them as a married couple. It wasn't exactly a good Christmas, even though they went out of their way to pretend otherwise."

"Was that before or after this?"

"Before, at least I think. I remember getting up and having a really good morning. At the time, I didn't realize what the blanket on the couch meant. I thought Dad was simply up early because he was excited for Christmas."

"Ah." Landon ran his hand over my back. "They were already gearing up for a separation. They didn't want to ruin your Christmas."

"Pretty much."

Mom and Dad continued to snipe at each other on the main floor as little Bay wandered through the room. Instead of stopping at the tree, as I expected, she moved to the bottom of the stairs and looked up. Her eyes locked with mine, and for a moment I thought I caught a glimpse of recognition on her face. It was gone before I could be sure.

"Who are you?"

I guess that answered that question. If little Bay could see us, that meant Mom and Dad could, too.

"I didn't realize we were having guests," Mom said, dragging her attention from Dad and focusing on Landon and me. She clearly didn't recognize me either, because the smile she pasted on her face was friendly and yet still remote. "I don't believe we've had the pleasure of being introduced."

"These are cousins," Aunt Tillie supplied, pinning me with a hard look. She practically dared me to tell Mom the truth and make things worse. "This is Daryl and Carol."

I couldn't stop myself from making a face. Daryl and Carol? Now she was just messing with us.

"And you're cousins?" Mom didn't look convinced.

"They are," Aunt Tillie confirmed. "Very distant cousins."

"Oh, from the Upper Peninsula?" Mom wrinkled her nose as she forced a grim smile.

Now Landon didn't realize it, but that was an insult. For years growing up, my cousins and I were inundated with stories about the loons living in the Upper Peninsula. To hear Aunt Tillie tell it, they ate raw meat off the bone, wandered around in public naked, and occasionally had sex with relatives to the point where they were dangerously close to running out of limbs on the family tree. We had no idea what that meant at the time. Once we grew older we were understandably intrigued – until we met them at one solstice celebration and realized the stories were not only true, but also woefully underplayed.

"We're not from the Upper Peninsula," I replied hurriedly. "We're from ... Detroit."

That wasn't much better in Mom's book – and her expression reflected just that – but she didn't panic and grab little Bay in an attempt to shield her, so I figured it would be okay.

"Oh, well, that's nice." Mom's smile never wavered, but she quickly lost interest in me. "I'll help you in the kitchen, Aunt Tillie. Marnie and Twila should be here any second to help, too."

"Sure." Aunt Tillie cast me a look as Landon and I stood at the bottom of the stairs. "Do you know why you're here?"

"Yes." I nodded without hesitation. "You want me to remember how miserable our Christmas was before you swooped in and saved us. I remember. Can we move on?"

"Not quite yet." Aunt Tillie cast a pointed look in little Bay's direction. "She's not ready for you to go."

"She's not ready?"

"You heard what I said."

I heaved a sigh. "Fine." I moved in little Bay's direction but stopped before Aunt Tillie could put too much distance between us. "By the way ... Daryl and Carol?"

Aunt Tillie shrugged, her mischievous smile back. "There was a marathon on last weekend."

"I know but ... ."

"It's fine," Landon said, grabbing my hand. "I always fancied myself Daryl anyway."

Aunt Tillie made a derisive sound in the back of her throat. "In your dreams."

I shook my head as I watched her go. She was enjoying this. That much was obvious. It wasn't like before, when she was tortured by memories. She was purposely inflicting this on us ... and loving every second of it.

"She's freaking evil," I muttered.

"I don't think that's the way to make it through this," Landon pointed out. "She clearly wants us to talk to you."

I slid him a sidelong look. "You just like seeing me when I was little."

"I do, and I'm not going to pretend otherwise," Landon said. "I like you at this age. It's when we run into your teenage self and you're still warm for my form that things get uncomfortable."

He had a point.

I didn't bother to hide my disdain for Dad when he made a groaning noise as he flipped up the foot stool on the chair and flicked between television stations rather than engage in conversation with little Bay. Granted, it wasn't as if he was being neglectful. In fact, what memories I had of that period proved him to be a fairly devoted father. The neglect didn't start until he moved away.

"Hey there, little missy." Landon offered up a charming smile for little Bay's benefit as we sat on the couch on the other side of the room. "Have you had a good Christmas?"

The other Bay nodded, her big blue eyes solemn. "Santa came."

"I bet he did." Landon slipped one of the girl's curls behind her ear. It was weird thinking of her as another entity, but it was even weirder to think of her as me. "What did you get?"

"I didn't get a dog." Younger Bay looked sad when she made the announcement. "I thought I was going to get one, but ... no."

"That's too bad," Landon said. "I'm sure you'll get one soon."

"I am, too," I supplied. "In fact, I'll bet you get a really great dog next year. The reason you couldn't get it this year is because the perfect dog for you hasn't been born yet."

Bay looked intrigued by the notion. "Do you really think so?"

I nodded. "I know so."

"Well, that's good. It makes me feel better." Even though she didn't know him, Bay climbed on the couch and settled next to Landon. She appeared perfectly comfortable in his company. "What did Santa bring you?"

"Oh, well ... ." Landon looked to me for help.

"He brought us a necklace and golf clubs," I replied, pulling two standard gifts out of thin air. "We're both really excited."

Bay made a face. "That sounds boring."

"You'll change your mind when you're older," Landon said, picking up Bay's hand so he could study it. Resting on his, it looked downright tiny. "What else did you ask Santa for?"

"Peace on Earth and good will toward men."

I pursed my lips at the rehearsed answer. "Really? How ... magnanimous of you."

"I don't know what that means, but I really asked for it," Bay said. "I want people to stop fighting. All people. So, I want peace on Earth. I told Aunt Tillie what I wanted and she said it was possible, and she always tells the truth."

It seemed little Bay was still a bit naïve. She hadn't caught on to Aunt Tillie's shenanigans yet. Still, I knew exactly what she meant in regard to fighting. I shifted my eyes to her father. He was my father, too, of course, but he was more her father than mine.

"Your next Christmas will be better," I promised, swallowing the lump in my throat. "At the time, you won't think so. Years from now, when you're old like us, you'll look back on it as one of the best Christmases ever."

Bay brightened considerably. "Do you really think so?"

"I really know."

"Okay." Little Bay patted Landon's knee before hopping off the couch. "I need to go to the bathroom. I'll be back."

"Okay," Landon called after her. "We'll be here."

"Not quite," Aunt Tillie countered, shaking her head. "You have somewhere else to be."

I furrowed my brow, confused. "And where is that?"

"Another Christmas celebration."

I opened my mouth to ask what she was talking about, but the room was already shifting, the Christmas from long ago gone and replaced by another. I recognized this one right away and couldn't stop my smile.

"Oh, now this is a better memory."

This travesty – or whatever it appeared to be – was officially looking up.

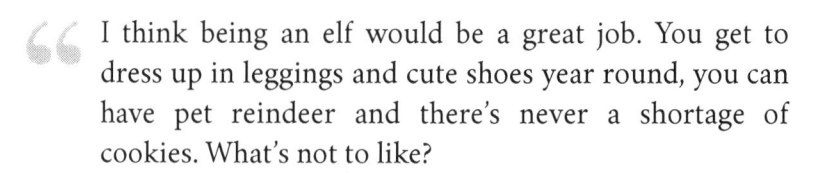

❝ I think being an elf would be a great job. You get to dress up in leggings and cute shoes year round, you can have pet reindeer and there's never a shortage of cookies. What's not to like?

— *C*love, 10, explaining what she wants to be when she grows up

FIVE

I recognized downtown Hemlock Cove right away, the overabundance of Christmas decorations serving as a fun reminder of holiday celebrations in my hometown. I slid a look to Aunt Tillie, excited despite myself.

"Are we about to see Sugar?"

Aunt Tillie shook her head. "Not quite yet. You have something else to do first."

It bothered me – and not just a little – that Aunt Tillie had seemingly cast herself as tour guide in this little fantasy. Our previous interactions with her in these worlds she created hadn't been remotely like this.

"What are we supposed to do first?" Landon asked.

"Visit an old friend." Aunt Tillie's smile was mischievous. "You're not quite done with the previous Christmas celebration. You need to visit one more person before we move on."

I was instantly suspicious. "Who? By the way, if you say it's Mrs. Little and you have something mean we're supposed to do to her, I'm totally going to find an empty booth in the diner and wait this out instead of participate."

"If you try to wait it out you'll never get out." Aunt Tillie said matter-of-factly. "You already know the rules of the game, Bay. You can't change them now."

"Yeah, but we're not playing the same game," I reminded her. "Before, in the fairy tale book, we had to make it to the end of the story and learn hard lessons about ourselves before escaping. This is something different. You said this wasn't about teaching us anything."

"What I said was that it was about punishing you for being a selfish little pain in my posterior," Aunt Tillie clarified. "I didn't say you wouldn't learn anything."

I narrowed my eyes. "What is it exactly that you're trying to do?"

"Save Christmas."

Aunt Tillie's answer was so simple I couldn't stop myself from staring. "Is Christmas in danger?"

"I guess you'll have to finish playing the game to find out," Aunt Tillie replied. "As I said earlier, you have to play the game to get credit for the win."

"You didn't say it that way," Landon argued, frowning as he smoothed the front of his coat. "It was bright red, puffy arms making him look wider than should be possible given his muscular frame. "What's up with the wardrobe choices, by the way? Can we put in requests for something less ... tacky?"

"I'll have you know I only pick out items that flatter," Aunt Tillie countered. "You, for example, have a puffed-out ego. You need a puffed-out jacket to go with it."

Landon heaved a sigh. "I should have seen that coming."

"You definitely should have," Aunt Tillie agreed. "Now, you two need to take a side trip while I ... um ... run an errand."

Run an errand? This was the weirdest Aunt Tillie world yet. "You're running errands at the same time you're torturing us in your brain's version of the North Pole?"

Aunt Tillie bobbed her head without hesitation. "You're not my only customers."

Something she said earlier dinged in my head. "Thistle and Clove," I muttered. "You have them in different versions of this game, don't you?"

"They're playing their own games, but they're no less important than the one you two are playing," Aunt Tillie replied. "I wasn't joking about you learning something while you find your Christmas spirit."

I balked. "We never lost our Christmas spirit. We made a mistake when we thought we wanted to spend Christmas alone. There's a difference."

"And yet you still haven't learned what that difference is," Aunt Tillie chided. "You need more punishment to do that."

I blew out a sigh, frustrated. "Fine. Will we eventually meet Thistle and Clove in this world?"

"Anything is possible."

I opened my mouth to bark at her, something harsh on the tip of my tongue. Landon stopped me with a hand on my arm and an almost imperceptible shake of his head.

"Where do you want us to go?" he asked, wrapping his fingers around my wrist to keep me still.

"You need to visit Terry," Aunt Tillie replied. "He's part of your Christmas story, although you won't see why right away."

I knit my eyebrows, confused. "This is the same Christmas we saw in your house, right?"

"Yes, but like you, not everyone had a merry Christmas that year."

"I don't know what that means," I pressed.

"Then I suggest you visit Terry and find out," Aunt Tillie suggested. "Don't forget, he lives in a different house now. Do you remember his old house?"

I racked my brain and nodded. "On Plum Street, not far from the playground."

"That's right." Aunt Tillie tilted her head to the side, as if listening to something only she could hear. "I really need to check on your cousins. Apparently Thistle isn't taking things nearly as well as I expected."

"How well did you expect her to take them?"

"Let's just say I searched high and low for a Christmas story to fit her needs and the only thing close I could come up with is *Black X-*

Mas," Aunt Tillie replied. "I had to make some ... tweaks ... for her. I don't think it's going over well."

I feigned amusement. "Well ... have a good time."

"I definitely will."

Aunt Tillie blinked out of existence, as if she'd never been there, and I couldn't stop myself from scanning the empty town square for a sign of her before speaking.

"This is weird."

"Really?" Landon arched a confrontational eyebrow. "What was your first clue?"

"Don't take that tone with me," I warned. "This isn't my fault."

"Which seems to mean you think it's my fault," Landon said. "I'm not sure how you can pin this one on me."

"You're the one who suggested we spend Christmas alone," I muttered under my breath, pointing myself in the direction of Chief Terry's former house.

"Hey, I didn't know how important Christmas was to Aunt Tillie. I never would've suggested it had I known. You did know, but you didn't say anything. I think that means this is your fault."

"Oh, well, good." I huffed. "I'm glad to see that we've finished the blame game for the day."

"You started it."

"And I didn't mean it," I shot back. "It slipped out. I'm simply ... frustrated."

Landon's expression softened as he captured my hand and fell into step with me. "Bay, we're in this together. This isn't the first time we've been trapped in ... well, whatever we're dealing with here. We'll get through it. We always do."

His words warmed me even as something he said tripped my recognition. "Except this isn't the same as before, at least not all the way," I noted. "Aunt Tillie said that Thistle and Clove were trapped in their own stories."

"I heard her. What do you think that means?"

"I don't know. We were living multiple stories in the fairy tale world."

"If I turn into a beast again I'm totally going to melt down."

I squeezed his hand, amused. "That turned out okay. I recognized you."

"Yeah, which still dumbfounds me," Landon admitted. "But let's go back to what you were saying. Do you think Clove and Thistle are trapped in this story with us?"

I gave the question serious thought before answering. "No. I think Aunt Tillie is running parallel punishments. You heard her. She said she wanted to send Thistle into *Black X-Mas*."

"I don't know what that is."

"It's a terrible horror movie set at an old house – I think it was a sorority house, if I'm not mistaken – and all these weird things start happening," I explained. "Eventually you find out the former owner's son is still hanging around, only he's yellow from lack of exposure to the sun and living in the walls of the house. He only pops out at night to kill people."

Landon blinked several times in rapid succession. "Do you really think Aunt Tillie sent Thistle there?"

"I wouldn't put it past her," I replied. "The thing is, Aunt Tillie never makes up anything from scratch. She always incorporates bits as inspiration. Even though she wrote her own fairy tale book, she used other stories as a basis and then twisted them to express whatever message she was most interested in that day."

"Okay, by that rationale, you're saying we're probably stuck in some version of a Christmas story or movie that Aunt Tillie enjoys," Landon said. "How long of a list is that?"

"Surprisingly long. She loves Christmas. She will watch any Christmas movie, even if it's bad."

"I figured that out when you told me what *Black X-Mas* was about," Landon said. "Still, she must have some favorites."

"She does." I searched my memory. "*Miracle on 34th Street*, *A Christmas Story*, *Elf*, *Love Actually* – oh, too bad we couldn't get that one, because then we could just hang around talking to one another in front of a tree – *It's a Wonderful Life*, *Home Alone*, *Scrooged*, *Bad Santa*."

"*Bad Santa*?" Landon was understandably horrified. "If you start sniffing around a filthy Santa carrying a pickle we're going to have a huge fight."

"I'll try to refrain," I said dryly. "I'm not sure which story she's dropped us in. So far we've seen only one Christmas memory and it wasn't exactly something that induced fond memories. That has to be deliberate."

"So why would she send us to Terry's house if that's the case?" Landon asked.

I shrugged, genuinely confused. "I don't know. I guess we'll find out." I pointed at the non-descript ranch house across the way. "He lives there."

"Okay, let's see what he's doing." Landon kept a firm grip on my hand as he led me across the snowy lawn. Instead of knocking, we planted ourselves in front of a window and peered inside. Landon was keen to keep our interaction with past versions of people we knew at a minimum, and I couldn't help but agree. I didn't think we were really in the past. It was more likely we were in a mirror version of the past so we wouldn't risk changing events. We still had to be careful, though.

"There he is," Landon said, pointing.

I followed Landon's finger and frowned when I saw Chief Terry – who wasn't the chief at this time, but I couldn't wrap my head around calling him something different – sitting in a chair by himself watching television. "What is he doing?"

Landon shrugged. "Chilling."

"But … it's Christmas."

"And?"

"And he's alone."

"Oh." Realization dawned on Landon. "I'm starting to think this Christmas thing isn't just Aunt Tillie. It's you, too."

"I didn't do this to us."

"No, but you're freaking out about a Christmas that was a good twenty-some years ago," Landon pointed out. "I'm sure Terry is just killing a few minutes before he leaves for a Christmas party or something."

I wasn't so sure. Chief Terry looked depressed. "We should talk to him." I moved to walk away from the window, but Landon stopped me.

"What are you going to say to him? Hi, I'm Bay from the future. You don't know it yet, but I'm going to complicate your life in ways that will regularly cause you to want to cry. Merry Christmas."

I scowled. "Was that your imitation of me?"

"Yes."

"I don't sound like that."

"That's exactly how you sound," Landon argued. "There's nothing you can say to him to make things better right now, Bay. This already happened."

"He's not wrong," Aunt Tillie said, popping into view. She wore the same outfit – a bright green coat, although it looked as if it had a fresh tear around one of her elbows that I was certain wasn't there a few minutes before – and her hair looked disheveled.

"Where have you been?" I asked.

"Checking on your cousins. They're fine, by the way. Clove sends her love and Thistle, well, Thistle blames you and sent you a big middle finger salute. I have a feeling it's going to take her the longest to work through her story."

There it was again. That word. *Story*. "What 'story' are we in?"

"That's for me to know and you to find out," Aunt Tillie replied. "Are you ready to see something else?"

"I'm still trying to figure out why you showed me this," I replied, glaring at Chief Terry's house. "This makes me sad."

"Christmas isn't always about being happy."

"It should be."

Aunt Tillie grinned. "I couldn't agree more. That's why we're moving this show along a bit."

Landon instinctively grabbed my hand as the background began to blur, but unlike our last trip through Aunt Tillie's mind we didn't land with a thump. Instead we magically appeared in the middle of the town square.

"We're back where we were a few minutes ago," Landon replied,

AMANDA M. LEE

glancing around. The square was packed with people. "It must be later in the day or something."

"No, it's a full year down the road," Aunt Tillie said. "Bay knows what will happen next. She thought that's what she was going to see when we first landed. Instead she got a detour."

"A depressing detour," I grumbled.

"Yes, and Terry is clearly fine now," Aunt Tillie said. "He'll be at the inn for Christmas, even if you two won't."

"I told you we were going to the inn for Christmas," I growled. "What more do you want?"

"I can't answer that. You need to figure it out for yourself." Aunt Tillie pointed when the sound of jingling bells and a loud "ho, ho, ho" pierced the air. "Here comes your favorite part."

Even though I was angry with Aunt Tillie I couldn't stop myself from snapping my head in that direction. Chief Terry, decked out in Santa's finest rented suit, made his way through the middle of town. Instinctively I flicked my eyes to the spot where I knew little me stood with my cousins. Landon grinned when he saw us, gripping my hand tighter.

"Look how cute you girls were."

"They weren't all that cute that Christmas," Aunt Tillie countered. "They were all pouty messes, especially this one." She jerked her thumb in my direction. "She wouldn't stop whining."

"I stopped whining eventually," I countered, my eyes misting when my younger counterpart approached Terry's sleigh. "Now shut up. I want to hear this."

Landon indulged me, slinking forward so we could listen to interaction from a Christmas long past.

"You must be Bay," Terry said, deepening his voice. "I hear you think Christmas is ruined this year."

Landon slid me a questioning look. "You thought Christmas was ruined?"

I waved off his question. "It's a long story."

Younger Bay stilled. "I ... who are you?" She had trouble putting a real face with the voice and beard. "I know you."

"Of course you know me," Terry said. "I'm Santa Claus! You don't believe in Santa Claus, though, do you?"

"No ... yes ... maybe ... ." Bay didn't know how to answer. "If you're Santa Claus, does that mean you brought me a gift?" She was testing the big man.

"I did."

"Even then you had him wrapped around your finger," Landon teased, grinning at Chief Terry's outfit.

"What is it?" Little Bay asked.

"You can't have it until I'm sure you believe in me," Terry replied. "Those are the rules."

Little Bay narrowed her eyes. "Who makes these rules?"

"My elves."

"Aren't you the boss of your elves?"

"I'm not the boss of anyone," Terry replied, his eyes landing on Aunt Tillie for a moment and then returning to young Bay's dubious face. "It seems everyone tells me what to do and I do it."

"That doesn't seem like a very good job," little Bay said.

"It's the best job in the world," Terry countered. "I'm Santa Claus. I get to bring joy to the world, even if people don't believe in me."

"He's laying it on a little thick," Landon whispered.

"No." My heart warmed as I witnessed the memory from a new vantage point. "He's laying it on just thick enough."

"Maybe I do believe in you," Young Bay hedged. "I ... ."

"If you believe in me, you have to say it," Terry prodded.

"I believe in you," young Bay mumbled.

"I can't hear you."

"She said she believes in you," Clove yelled, causing Landon to snicker.

"Thank you, Clove," Terry said. "I know you believe. Your present will be coming as soon as Bay tells me she believes."

It was the moment of truth. Young Bay knew it. Everyone in town knew it. Now she only had to admit it.

"Fine," little Bay said, crossing her arms over her chest. "I believe in Santa Claus."

"I still can't hear you," Terry said, staring her down. "You need to say it louder!"

"I believe in Santa Claus!" young Bay practically screamed the words and Terry broke out in a huge grin.

"That's better," Terry said, leaning over and rummaging in the bag at his feet. When he turned around, he held a puppy. The black cutie had a huge bow tied around its neck and it wriggled crazily.

Little Bay's eyes widened as she took another step forward. "Is that for me?"

"That's for you, Clove and Thistle," Terry replied.

Young Bay took the puppy, her eyes filling with tears. "Thank you."

"You have to take care of him," Terry said. "You girls have to feed him and walk him and love him. Do you think you're up to the task?"

"You bet we are," Clove said, rushing to younger Bay's side so she could pet the puppy. "Wow!"

"How did you know to get us a puppy?" little Bay asked.

"One of my elves told me."

"How did the elf know?"

"Your Aunt Tillie has a huge mouth," Terry replied, smiling at young Bay one more time before turning his attention to the rest of the children. "Who wants presents?"

The squeals were deafening as they surged in around him. Terry didn't put up a fight as they started climbing on his lap and telling him their most fervent wishes.

I risked a glance at Landon and found him swiping at what he would later claim to be an imaginary tear. "You look a little misty."

"I simply have something in my eye."

I wasn't convinced. "You should probably get it out."

"That's the plan."

I slid a glance in Aunt Tillie's direction. "This is one of my favorite Christmas memories. Thank you."

"It's one of mine, too." Aunt Tillie gestured toward the spot where her alter ego talked with Mom and the other Bay. "You're over there telling me that I have to help you name the puppy. You didn't really let me help, though. Trust me. I wouldn't have named him Sugar."

"I thought this Christmas would be the worst ever, but it was really better than the previous one," I noted. "I think that was the point of this little visit, though, right?"

"I have multiple points." Aunt Tillie's grin was mischievous as she focused on Landon.

"Speaking of that, Bay isn't the only one who has something special to see."

"What does that mean?" Landon asked, suspicious.

Aunt Tillie held her hands palms up. "Let's find out, shall we?"

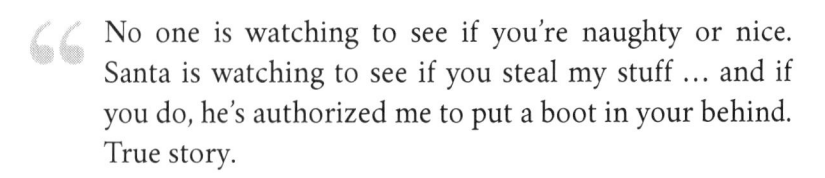

> No one is watching to see if you're naughty or nice. Santa is watching to see if you steal my stuff … and if you do, he's authorized me to put a boot in your behind. True story.
>
> — Aunt Tillie explaining the Christmas season to her young great-nieces

SIX

❄

I didn't recognize the next location. Not even a little. Apparently Landon did, though, because he immediately released my hand when he caught sight of the house that materialized in front of us.

"No way!"

I watched Landon, curious, and followed him as he hopped to the front walkway. He grinned as he pointed to a trio of snowmen on the front lawn. "The middle one is mine."

"Oh, well ... fun." I spared a glance for Aunt Tillie. "This is Landon's house?"

"It's his parents' house," Aunt Tillie said. "I guess it was his home for eighteen years. He seems excited, doesn't he?"

One look at my boyfriend, his face flushed with color, told me he'd completely forgotten about the tears he almost shed when visiting a memory from my past. "He does. This is a nice touch."

"Oh, it's going to get nicer." Aunt Tillie squared her shoulders as she walked up the sidewalk and knocked on the door.

"What are you doing?" I hissed, scurrying behind her. "Won't talking to them mess up the past?"

"We're not traveling through time, Bay," Aunt Tillie said dryly. "That's impossible."

I wasn't so sure. I knew our former jaunt through the decades only happened in Aunt Tillie's mind, but she convinced me at a young age that she could accomplish almost anything. "Are you sure?"

"Oh, just ... suck it up. You're an adult. Act like one."

The door opened, revealing Connie Michaels, Landon's mother. She looked younger – a good twenty years younger, at least – but her smile was evergreen and her eyes sparkled when they landed on Aunt Tillie.

"You're late!"

Late? Did that mean Connie expected us? How could that be? "What's going on?"

Aunt Tillie ignored the question. "I smell dinner cooking."

"Yes, I've been slaving for hours." Connie's gaze landed on me. "You brought guests."

"I told you I would."

"You should probably make introductions," Connie suggested.

"Right you are." Aunt Tillie tossed a glance over her shoulder to where Landon continued to marvel at the snowmen. "Hey, copper, get your behind over here."

Landon reluctantly left his childhood masterpiece behind and jogged to the front door. When he caught sight of his mother, he let loose a sound I couldn't quite identify and pulled her in for a bear hug. "I can't believe it's you!"

Instead of hugging Landon as if she recognized him, Connie awkwardly patted his back and exchanged an odd look with Aunt Tillie. "And I can't believe it's you."

"Stop being a schmuck," Aunt Tillie ordered, grabbing Landon by the ear and dragging him back. "She'll think you're a pervert or something."

Landon was understandably affronted. "That's gross. She's my mother, for crying out loud."

"Well, remember who you are," Aunt Tillie stressed. "Also, remember when you are."

Landon was appropriately abashed. "Sorry."

"Don't worry about it," Connie said, waving off Landon's concern. "You need to introduce us, Tillie. I'm going to need something to call these two or it's going to get awkward very quickly."

"Wait ... they know each other?" Landon glanced to me for confirmation. "How does that work?"

That was a very good question. "I have no idea. Just go with it. Aunt Tillie is up to something big, and we won't figure out what until we play the game."

"Good girl," Aunt Tillie said. "You're finally thinking." She fixed her attention on Connie. "This is Harold and Maude. They're cousins of sorts."

Harold and Maude? Really? "What happened to Daryl and Carol?" I asked.

Aunt Tillie shot me a "well, duh" look. "There's already a Daryl in this house."

Oh, well, she wasn't wrong. One of Landon's brothers was named Daryl. He was probably inside right now, although much younger. "Right."

"Why Harold and Maude?" Landon asked.

"It's one of Aunt Tillie's favorite movies," I replied. "I'll show it to you one day."

"Will I like it?"

"Probably not. It seems to be a movie only women love. I can't explain it."

"What are you talking about?" Connie asked, her placid smile never vacating her face.

"Nothing," Aunt Tillie replied. "We're here to enjoy Christmas. Lead the way."

Landon seemed nervous as his mother – who wasn't technically his mother in this case – ushered him inside his childhood home. He glanced around, his eyes wide with wonder, and grinned when he pointed at the mistletoe hanging over the doorframe that led to the living room.

"You want to do that now?" I couldn't help but be dubious.

"No. We used to make groaning noises whenever Mom and Dad did, though. When you have a house full of boys, stuff like that is strictly forbidden."

"And now?"

Landon smacked a quick but noisy kiss against my mouth. "Now it's recommended."

"Nice."

This was Landon's domain, so I followed him into the living room, where a trio of excited boys watched their father stare at a set of instructions. Earl Michaels, Landon's father, seemed oblivious to the new guests.

"Come on, Dad," one of the younger boys whined. "You said you were going to put it together so we could play with it."

"That's Denny," Landon noted, his voice low. "He was always a whiner."

"Then that must mean he's Daryl," I said, pointing toward a second boy. This one looked much more disinterested in the process than Denny.

Landon nodded. "Yeah. Remember that train set I told you about?"

"Yes."

"That's it."

"Oh, well, fun."

"It will take him the entire day to put it together," Landon said, keeping his voice low as he led me to the floral print couch at the center of the room. "The kids will lose interest – they mostly have now – but they'll have it for a really long time and never forget how much fun they had with their father while playing with it."

Landon sounded almost whimsical.

"I'm glad we got to see something from your past this time." I meant it. "Why aren't you involved? I mean … young Landon." It was weird to consider the dark-haired boy in the corner separately from the man sitting next to me.

"I believe I'm pouting because I wanted a new video game system," Landon replied. "Don't worry. I get over it fairly quickly."

The boy, little Landon, caught my eye. It was almost as if he sensed we were talking about him.

"Boys, come over here so I can make introductions," Connie ordered, wiping her hands on her apron.

Denny and Daryl immediately did as instructed, shuffling to Connie's side and eyeing us quizzically.

"This is Denny and Daryl." Connie beamed at her boys. "Landon, come over here."

My Landon jolted at the sound of his name, but he didn't go to his mother. Instead he turned to the boy in the corner and waited.

Little Landon looked to have a lot of attitude. He heaved a dramatic sigh and moved to Connie's side. The look he spared for Landon was one of disinterest. The one he planted on me was somehow different.

"This is Landon," Connie said, fussing with the boy's hair. "He's in a bit of a mood."

"What happened?" Aunt Tillie asked the boy. "Didn't you get what you wanted from Santa?"

"Nope." Little Landon crossed his arms over his chest, irritated. "I wanted the new PlayStation and instead I got ... that." He offered a vague wave to the train set Earl fixated on. "I didn't want that."

"Why?" I asked. "I'd think a train set is cooler than a video game system. You'll enjoy that set for years to come."

Young Landon rolled his eyes, mimicking an expression I often saw on his older counterpart's face. "Then you don't get how much cooler video games are."

"They really are cool," Aunt Tillie enthused. "But trains are cool, too."

Little Landon was dismissive. "Whatever." He turned his full attention to me. "Why are you here? I've never heard my mom mention you."

He had an inquisitive mind, even as a youngster. It made me smile. He was interrogating me and he didn't even know it. I wasn't sure why he picked me – maybe he figured my fond smile made me an easy mark – but I was glad for the attention. "We were passing through town and Aunt Tillie decided she needed to stop by," I explained. "It was a spur-of-the-moment thing."

"But you're not from around here?"

"No. We're from ... up north."

"The Upper Peninsula?"

"No, more by Traverse City. Do you know where that is?"

Little Landon shook his head. His hair was much shorter, the dark locks a sharp contrast to his olive skin. The blue of his eyes was so vibrant it almost made him look like a magical fairy creature. It was a ridiculous thought, yet I couldn't shake it.

"It's about two hours from here," Earl supplied, his gaze fixated on the train set instructions. "If I didn't know better, I'd think these instructions were written in another language."

Landon shot me a questioning look. I knew what he was asking. He wanted permission to work on the train set with his father. It would enhance the memories he already had of the train. I nodded without hesitation, grinning as I watched him move to the floor. When I finally tore my gaze from him, I found little Landon watching me with an unreadable gaze.

"What were we talking about again?"

"What you're doing here," the boy answered, surprising me when he settled in the spot Landon occupied moments before. "I don't think I know you, but I feel like I do."

"Oh, well ... ." In truth, I wasn't sure how that could be either. "Why do you think I'm familiar?"

"I don't know." Little Landon's eyes focused on my hair and he lifted a hand and touched it. "I think maybe I dreamed about you."

It should've been an innocent statement, something sweet and cute, but it gave me a jolt. "You've dreamed about me?"

"Oh, here we go," Daryl muttered, rolling his eyes as he moved to join his father. "He's going to start telling you about his weird dreams. They're so boring."

"They're not boring," Denny countered. "I think they mean something." Even as a child, Denny had a calm demeanor that I found quite appealing. He would grow up to be a minister, something that made me nervous when I first met him, but he had a mild and congenial way of interacting with others.

"What kind of dreams?" I asked.

"He dreams about angels," Denny replied.

"They're not angels," young Landon countered. "They're ... something else."

I was understandably fascinated. "What?"

"I don't ... ." The boy was earnest. "I can't really remember the dreams when I wake up. I remember little ... um ... bits of them. I don't remember all of them."

"I still think they're angels," Denny said.

Aunt Tillie snorted. "You would."

I shot her a warning look. "They probably are angels. Maybe they're just a different type of angel."

"I didn't know there were different kinds," Denny admitted.

"Nobody is ever just one thing," I said, grappling for words that he'd understand. He seemed wise beyond his years, but he was still a child. "People are many things. I think that means there can be different types of angels."

Denny seemed fine with the explanation. "Cool." He wandered over to Landon and Earl, dropping to his knees so he could watch them work. He appeared to be much more interested in what they were doing rather than the conversation between me and Landon's younger self.

"How long have you been having the dreams?" I asked, holding back my itchy fingers because they longed to run through little Landon's hair. Not in a creepy way, mind you, but it was so weird seeing Landon's childhood visage sitting next to me that it took everything I had not to touch him so that I could commit things – like the feeling of his hair – to memory.

"I don't know," the boy replied. He didn't seem agitated by the question, but he wasn't exactly engaged either. "I just have them sometimes." His eyes locked with mine. "I'm sure you were there."

"What did I do?"

"You talked to me. You … smiled. I think there might have been bacon."

I pressed my lips together to keep from laughing and slid a curious look in Aunt Tillie's direction. "Did you make him say that?"

Aunt Tillie shook her head. "He says what he wants. I only brought you here. What's happening is real. Er, well, at least as real as it can be."

I was surprised. "Does that mean … ?"

"What? Are you asking if he dreamed of you before he ever met you?" Aunt Tillie shrugged, her lips curving. "Anything is possible, right?"

This night was certainly proof of that.

"I KNOW IT'S A dream, but it was nice having Christmas dinner with my family."

Landon stood with me under the mistletoe two hours later, his arm slung around my shoulders. He looked happy, well fed and utterly amused by everything happening in the next room.

I followed his gaze, grinning when I saw Denny and Daryl wrestling for the turkey wishbone. "I'm glad I got to see you as a kid for a change," I said. "You're so cute."

"I think you're only saying that because I find little Bay so adorable."

"No, I really like little Landon," I countered. "He told me something odd, though. Did you hear what we were talking about?"

Landon shook his head. "No. I was too busy talking to my father. It was weird to be able to hang with him that way. I kind of got distracted."

"I wouldn't begrudge you time with your father for anything," I said. "I mean that."

"I know." Landon kissed the tip of my nose, eliciting gagging sounds from the three boys in the dining room. He chuckled when he heard them. "Ah, that brings back memories."

"I think this entire trip is supposed to bring back memories," I pointed out. "That's why Aunt Tillie brought us here."

"And I thought she brought us here to punish us." Landon pressed a soft kiss to the corner of my mouth as he held me close to his chest. "I'm not feeling punished."

"Give it time," Aunt Tillie said, breezing past us as she moved between the bathroom and the dining room.

Landon watched her go, a mixture of baffled amusement and suspicion flitting across his face. "I don't understand what she's trying to prove to us. This was more a gift than anything else."

"Yeah, I wouldn't get too cocky. She can shift us to another memory – one that's not quite so good – at any moment. The fact that she let us stay here so long, that we enjoyed ourselves, makes me think our next stop will be a nightmare."

"I don't care." Landon rested his cheek against my forehead. "I'm glad I got to share this with you."

"I'm glad, too." I really was. "It makes me realize that our lives weren't really that different."

Landon pulled back so he could study my face. "Did you think they were?"

I shrugged. "I grew up with witches."

"So?"

"I thought you had a more normal childhood. Now I'm not so sure."

"I don't know what that means."

"You grew up with dreams."

Landon stilled, his hand slowing as he rubbed the back of my neck. "Dreams?"

I searched his face for a hint of recognition. "Or maybe you didn't," I conceded. "Aunt Tillie said that everything happening was real. I probably shouldn't have believed her. That was wishful thinking on my part."

"Not necessarily," Landon hedged. "I just … I did use to have dreams. They were about angels."

My heart rate picked up a notch. "Yes. That's what Denny said."

"I forgot all about them," Landon admitted. "I stopped having them when I turned about eleven or twelve. I can't really remember."

"Do you remember what the dreams were about now?"

"No. I never remembered. They were just bright glimpses of ... something. I remember a lot of blonde hair." He absently stroked his hand down the back of my head. "It's weird that little me brought that up to you."

"He said I looked familiar."

"Really?" Landon cocked an eyebrow. "Maybe I was dreaming about you instead of an angel."

I knew he didn't mean it as a slight, but I couldn't help being a bit bothered. "I could be an angel!"

"No, you're my sweetie." Landon kissed my cheeks, but his expression was distant. "That's really odd. Where is he? I mean, where am I? It's still weird to talk about my younger self that way."

"It doesn't matter," Aunt Tillie said, popping up at my side. "You've learned all you're going to here."

"I want to talk to him," Landon pressed.

"You'll get another chance," Aunt Tillie promised. "In fact ... ." She shifted her eyes to the grandfather clock as it began dinging. "In fact, I think you're about to get another shot."

"What does that mean?"

Aunt Tillie didn't answer. It was already too late. The room swirled, and we were off on yet another adventure. My gut told me the next one wouldn't be nearly as pleasant.

> You'll shoot your eye out.

— *Landon* to Aunt Tillie when she takes her shotgun turkey hunting

SEVEN

The swirling didn't last long, and when it ended, we were right back in front of the same house. It was different – the trim a bright blue instead of a muted green – but the ambiance was largely the same.

"Did something go wrong?" I asked, glancing around.

Aunt Tillie shook her head. "We're right where we're supposed to be."

"And where is that?"

"Where is not the right question. When is the right question."

Ugh. Now she was playing semantics in an effort to drive me crazy. "Okay. When are we?"

"In the past."

"Do you want to be more specific?"

"Not really." Aunt Tillie's grin was all sorts of evil. "We're here because Landon needs to be reminded of when he lost his Christmas spirit."

Landon groaned as he pinched the bridge of his nose. "I have not lost my Christmas spirit. Is that what you think?"

"That's what I know."

"It's not true," Landon snapped. "I have plenty of Christmas spirit.

In fact, I have Christmas spirit coming out of my … ."

Aunt Tillie extended a warning finger. "Don't say anything vulgar. It's Christmas."

"I was going to say earholes," Landon growled. "When do I say vulgar things?"

"When you're alone with Bay and think no one is listening."

"Wait … ." Something occurred to me. "How do you know that?"

"I know everything," Aunt Tillie replied. "When will you realize that?"

"I don't say vulgar things to her." Landon was only partially talking to us. Most of his attention seemed to be focused internally. "I say flirty things. There's a difference."

"Not in my world," Aunt Tillie said. "Your version of flirty is another man's version of hard time in state prison."

Landon tilted his head to the side, his glossy black hair slipping below his shoulder. "How do you figure that?"

"Ignore her," I prodded. "She's trying to unnerve you."

"She's doing a good job."

"That's why she's Aunt Tillie." I moved to step from the snowbank I found myself lodged in and struggled toward the front walk, frowning when I caught sight of my boots. "What are these?" I'm not one for fashion meltdowns, but my current footwear was beyond mortifying.

"They're boots," Aunt Tillie replied simply.

"They have fur on them."

"Not real fur. I didn't kill a bear or anything."

That didn't make me feel much better. "I look as if I'm wearing Chewbacca's legs or something." The boots reached almost to my knees and the brown fur was acrylic … and tacky.

Landon followed my gaze, amused. "They're kind of cute."

That wasn't the word I would use for them. "People are going to mistake me for Bigfoot and shoot me."

"Oh, don't be such a kvetch." Aunt Tillie rolled her eyes. "I thought Clove was being a kvetch in her story until now. Geez! Get over it."

"Speaking of Clove, where is she? Are we going to run into

her soon?"

"I sincerely doubt that you'll run into Clove," Aunt Tillie said. "Her punishment is different from yours."

That didn't sound good. "Meaning?"

"Meaning that you don't have to worry about Clove," Aunt Tillie replied. "She's ... holding her own."

Landon and I exchanged a quick look as Aunt Tillie made her way to the sidewalk.

"That sounded ominous, right?"

Landon shrugged. "I don't think Aunt Tillie would go so far as to risk Clove's life."

"That doesn't mean Clove isn't in danger. Do you remember the fairy tale world?"

"Do you have to keep bringing that up?"

"I'm just saying ... the danger felt very real when we were trapped in the book," I said. "Wherever Clove is, the danger might feel very real to her."

"The danger feels very real to Clove when she's shaving her legs," Aunt Tillie drawled. "The girl is a dramatic pain in the keister. She's fine, though. I have everything under control."

I had my doubts. Still, Aunt Tillie was in charge. It wasn't as if we could shake ourselves from our current predicament, so we had to rely on her to save us. "Why are we here?"

"Because I wanted Landon to get a gander of the man he almost was," Aunt Tillie replied. "He forgot the dreams, although they weren't important when it came to shaping him. I'm guessing he forgot this, too."

"Forgot what?" Landon asked, moving closer to me. "I didn't forget the dreams as much as I ... just didn't remember."

"I fail to see the difference," Aunt Tillie argued.

"You're really on my last nerve," Landon muttered, shaking his head. "Go ahead. Show me."

"I won't be showing you anything," Aunt Tillie countered. "This one you have to figure out on your own. I'll simply be supervising the experience."

"Supervising what?" I asked, glancing around.

As if on cue, a tacky orange Camaro roared to a stop in front of the house, the driver locking the brakes and causing the vehicle to skid. Landon whipped his head in the direction of the street, his lips curving down.

"Uh-oh."

"Uh-oh what?" I was unbelievably curious.

Landon turned a set of accusatory eyes in Aunt Tillie's direction. "You did this on purpose."

"I'm not doing anything," Aunt Tillie clarified. "I'm simply following where the Christmas memories take me."

"You're evil."

I couldn't understand Landon's reaction to the appearance of the ugly car. "Do you know who's in there?" I squinted as I peered toward the vehicle. "It has to be some middle-aged man going through a mid-life crisis. Who else would buy a car like that?"

"Bay … ." Landon didn't get a chance to finish whatever he was going to say because the passenger side door exploded with activity, a lithe blonde with overblown hair and a faux fur coat exiting. She looked to be loaded for bear.

"I hate you!" She screeched at the car, momentarily making me wonder if the vehicle was somehow possessed. Perhaps we were in our own version of a horror movie after all.

"Shelly Waterman," Landon muttered, shaking his head. "Oh, my … ."

"Do you know her?" I was understandably curious. "Is she a cousin or something?" It was a stupid question. In hindsight, I would realize that his reaction was too primal for the girl to be anything other than what she ultimately turned out to be. I was purposely blind to it, though. I didn't want to see what was right in front of me.

"Okay, I've learned my lesson." Landon turned to Aunt Tillie, a pleading look on his face. "I will never suggest spending time away from you on Christmas again. I've been sufficiently punished. Take us home."

Aunt Tillie, clearly enjoying her position as power forward for the

Winchester witches' basketball team, made a clucking sound with her tongue. "I kind of want to see what happens."

She wasn't the only one. "Who is Shelly Waterman?"

Landon was at a loss for words. "I just … ."

"Did you hear me?" Shelly bellowed to the car. "I hate you!"

I watched with interest as the car engine died and the driver's side door popped open. The individual who climbed out was straight out of teenage Bay's dreams. He had long black hair – even longer than the current model – and a letterman jacket draping his square shoulders. His blue eyes were piercing as they scanned the front yard – lingering an additional moment when they met mine – and then he focused on the pretty blonde.

"Chill out," teenage Landon ordered, his keys jingling as he slammed shut the car door.

"Oh, my … ."

"Don't say it," Landon muttered, slapping his hand over his eyes. "I can't look."

"You've already seen all of this," Aunt Tillie reminded him. "You lived it. You … rocked it." She was having far too good a time. I thought there was a legitimate chance Landon might gag her to end the yammering in his head.

"So … that's you as a teenager, huh?" I forced a smile. I was trying to make things easier for him, although I had no idea why. I couldn't stop staring at the boy strolling up the sidewalk.

"I'm not joking with you," Shelly screeched. "I hate your guts! I know what you were doing with Deanna Hardy under the bleachers. Three different people told me."

"I think they must've mistaken me for someone else." Teenage Landon was cool under pressure. He didn't look worried that Shelly would break up with him – or worse, kill him. He seemed more agitated than anything else. "It wasn't me."

I slid a sidelong look to my Landon. "Was it you?"

Landon nodded. "I had … issues."

"I'll say you had issues," Aunt Tillie cackled. "What is up with that hair?"

"I'll have you know that my hair was quite popular back then," Landon challenged. "Women everywhere fell over themselves to run their fingers through it."

"Obviously," I said dryly, doing my best to pretend we weren't interlopers watching two teenagers carry out some odd scene from a future episode of *Days of Our Lives*. "I'm starting to get the idea that you were very popular in high school."

"I was ... easy to get along with," Landon hedged.

"I don't believe you," Shelly snapped. "You were supposed to be watching me play volleyball for the charity Christmas tournament and you disappeared all day. Deanna disappeared, too, and she wasn't wearing a bra when she came back!"

I felt sick to my stomach. Sure, in my head I knew that she was talking to teenage Landon – who was years from turning into the man I'd meet and ultimately fall in love with – but I never considered him a dog while we were dating. That's the only word that seemed to describe the young tough sauntering up the front walk.

"It's not my fault Deanna lost her bra," the younger Landon argued. "I don't have it. I don't know why you're blaming me."

"You were supposed to be watching me play volleyball," Shelly challenged.

"Volleyball isn't really a sport," the teenage boy argued. "It's great in the Olympics when the women are wearing those skimpy bikinis – even if most of them are flat chested – but it's pretty boring when done on a team. I know it's not your fault. Chicks don't play real sports. Still ... I had to walk around or I would've fallen asleep."

My mouth dropped open as I turned a dark stare on adult Landon. He shifted uncomfortably from one foot to the other, refusing to make eye contact.

"I can't believe you just said that," I hissed.

"Yes, well, I told you he had issues," Landon gritted out. "He wasn't a nice kid."

"You mean you weren't a nice kid."

"I mean that I was full of myself and I didn't grow into the idea of what a real man was supposed to be until long after I graduated from high school," Landon said. "I was a … um … I'm not sure what word I would use to describe me."

"Turd," Aunt Tillie offered helpfully.

Landon scowled. "I wouldn't use that word."

"I would," I muttered, turning back to the couple.

"I really can't stand you right now," Shelly sniffed, her lower lip trembling. I wasn't a fan of Landon's teenage form, but her overreaction made me roll my eyes. "You're breaking my heart."

"It looks like it's working to me," younger Landon said dryly, stopping in front of his future self and looking him up and down. The fact that my Landon was dressed in red corduroy pants and an ugly Santa sweater wasn't lost on him. "Who are you?"

"You don't want to know," Landon growled, shaking his head.

"Did you hear the way he was talking to me?" Shelly asked, turning her glassy eyes in my direction. "He's mean and terrible. You heard him, right?"

"We heard him," I conceded. "He was … unpleasant. That's no reason to cry, though."

"He's the love of my life," Shelly wailed. "He was supposed to spend Christmas with me and my parents, but he changed his mind at the school and now we have to do what he wants. He's a terrible boyfriend."

"Then why are you with him?"

Given the look on Shelly's face, I wasn't sure the question registered. "What do you mean? Look at him."

I'd had my fill of looking at *The Breakfast Club* wannabe. "You'll find someone better. Trust me."

"Hey!" Landon shot me a look.

I sucked in a breath to calm myself. It wasn't Landon's fault, after all. He was a teenager. Teenagers do moronic and hurtful things all the time without realizing the ramifications of their actions. Still, I couldn't hide my disgust.

"Don't worry about him, Shelly." I chose my words carefully. "He's not good enough for you, and by the time he is good enough for you … well … he'll be with someone else."

"Like who?" Shelly planted her hands on her narrow hips. "If you say Deanna, I'll start throwing punches."

"Do that anyway," younger Landon suggested, giving his older counterpart a saucy wink. "I love it when chicks fight and rip each other's clothes off, don't you?"

"And … we're done here." Landon grabbed my hand. "I think we've seen more than enough of this particular show, Aunt Tillie."

"Oh, now, I thought we'd stay until the little punk gets antsy and breaks up with her," Aunt Tillie argued. "It's very entertaining."

"You break up with her on Christmas?" I was incredulous as I asked the question of adult Landon.

"I can't remember the specifics," Landon muttered.

"I do," Aunt Tillie offered. "He breaks up with her and goes inside to eat dinner with his family. She stays out here for the entire meal – threatening to get swine flu from the cold and everything – and then cries for two straight hours before calling her father to give her a ride home."

"You couldn't even give her a ride home?"

"You don't understand," Landon protested. "She was unbelievable work. I didn't even really like her. She was too much work for any teenager, let alone a disinterested one like me. She wasn't worth it – not like you are."

That should've made me feel better, yet I didn't rein in my scolding. "Landon, she's a teenager. All teenagers are dramatic."

"Why is the hot blonde calling you my name?" teenage Landon asked, confused.

Landon waved a finger in the boy's face. "She's not hot! Don't even think about looking at her."

I couldn't stop myself from being insulted. "Hey!"

"I didn't mean that the way it came out," Landon whined, lobbing a pleading look in my direction. "Of course I think you're hot. You're mine. I think you're the hottest woman in the world."

That should've made me feel marginally better, but it didn't.

"It's just … he's a walking hormone," Landon argued. "He'll try to put the moves on you."

"How do you know that?"

"Because I would've tried to put the moves on you."

"What is going on here?" Shelly asked, raising her chin. "Is this some sort of prank? Is that what's going on? That would explain so much."

"It's not a prank," Landon snapped. "You need to go home and get over yourself. By the way, when I say 'get over yourself,' I don't mean come up with a ridiculous plan to shave Deanna bald. That's going to get you suspended."

Shelly narrowed her eyes. "Who told you that?"

"I think something weird is going on here," younger Landon said. "In fact, I'm pretty sure this guy is crazy. I think you should give the blonde to me – just for safe keeping and all – and I'll have my father call the police so they can make sure you get back on your meds."

Aunt Tillie slapped Landon's arm as she chuckled. "You were a sarcastic pain in the butt even then, weren't you?"

Landon murdered her with a glare. "You've made your point. I don't want to be here any longer. Get us out of here."

Aunt Tillie squinted one eye as she regarded him. "Are you sure? There's plenty more fun where this came from."

"I'm unbelievably sure," Landon barked, grabbing my arm and pressing my body against his chest as he shot his teenage self a warning look. "Don't even think about it."

Younger Landon adopted an innocent expression. "What do you think I'm going to do?"

"I know exactly what you're going to try to do."

"How?"

"Because ... I just do." Landon wrapped his arms tightly around my back. "Get us out of here."

Aunt Tillie sighed. "Okay, but things were just starting to get fun."

I couldn't help being relieved when the swirling returned. Whatever memory we hopped to next had to be better than this.

Right?

" Other people don't get the Grinch, but I do. I think the Grinch had the right idea. He stole the gifts, and all the people of Whoville sang anyway. What he should've done is steal all the gifts and punch them each in the throat before leaving town. That would've handled that singing problem.

— *Thistle getting into the Christmas spirit*

EIGHT

I woke with a start, bolting upright in my own bed and staring into the gloominess of my bedroom. Landon slept next to me, the rhythmic sound of his breathing serving as comfort despite the extremely odd dream I'd just ripped myself from.

Was it really a dream, though?

I considered waking Landon to compare notes, but he looked so comfortable it seemed unnecessary. Surely if he dreamed the same thing I did he would've woken at the same time.

I scratched my shoulder, my eyes drifting to my pajamas. It was the middle of winter so I usually opted for fuzzy sleep pants and a T-shirt, something Landon never complained about or commented on. I shifted my eyes to the window closest to the bed. I could see snow falling and expected a heavy blanket of powdery white wonder to greet me with the dawn in a few hours. The sun was hours from rising and the moon was obliterated by clouds and snow, the view through the window hazy and dreamy.

I spared another glance for Landon. He hadn't as much as shifted to signify discomfort let alone wakefulness. I knew I wouldn't immediately be able to fall back to sleep, so I left Landon alone in the bedroom – quietly securing the door to make sure he wasn't roused when I turned on a light – and settled in the living room to think about the dream.

In truth, I wasn't sure it was a dream. Aunt Tillie was prone to messing with our minds – even dreams – when it suited her. This could surely be a case of that. I'd been feeling guilty about blowing off my family's Christmas Day traditions right before bed, so the dream might've been a manifestation of guilt.

It might've been real, too.

A soft knock at the door caused me to stare in that direction, my heart racing. It was well after midnight. Who would possibly come calling at this hour? The answer slammed into me almost instantly. If the dream was real, then perhaps Clove and Thistle were forced into some dark story, too. One of them might be coming to check on us.

I didn't bother to grab a robe before walking to the door, and given how dark it was outside there was no sense looking through the peephole. For one brief moment I thought that might possibly be the worst mistake I ever made when I saw the tall figure standing on the other side of the threshold.

Something terrible was about to happen, and Landon wouldn't be able to stop it because he was asleep.

I opened my mouth to yell, to at least alert him so he could save himself from attack. The man standing on the porch didn't allow me the option, though.

"Are you going to invite me in, Bay?"

I recognized the voice. Not from my life, of course, but from a different sort of memory. Dumbfounded, I pushed opened the door and stepped away to grant Uncle Calvin access.

"What are you doing here?"

It was an absolutely moronic question. However, I couldn't think of what else to say.

Uncle Calvin merely chuckled as he closed the door, giving the guesthouse a quick study before focusing on me. "Merry Christmas to you, too!"

"Merry Christmas," I corrected hurriedly. "What are you doing here?"

"I'm here to see you."

"Why?"

"Why not?"

"Is this a dream?" I was understandably suspicious. Perhaps Landon didn't wake up because Aunt Tillie intended to separate us for the second leg of our punishment. It was the only thing that made sense.

"I'm dead," Uncle Calvin reminded me, walking to the chair at the end of the room so he could settle his lanky frame. "The dead don't dream."

"Really?" I found the tidbit intriguing. "What do you do?"

"Watch those we love. If they happen to be with us, then we hang out and watch television and listen to music."

"Really?"

Uncle Calvin chuckled. "No, but if the people we love are with us we can enjoy a variety of different outings. I just happen to be waiting for the person I love most."

Even though it was a surreal situation, I relished the chance to talk to the man who whispered in my ear on occasion. My witchy gift is talking to the dead, so when things got tough or Aunt Tillie threatened to go off the rails, her late husband's spirit occasionally showed up to help me fix things. I never saw him – other than the trip through Aunt Tillie's memories – but we'd chatted a time or two.

"Does that make you sad?"

"What?"

"Having to stay there – wherever you are – without Aunt Tillie?"

"I miss her, but I understand it's not her time yet. Why? Do you want me to take her with me?"

That was an interesting question. "Before tonight I would've said no. Right now? I'm not so sure. This is all part of that demented mind of hers, right?"

"Yes and no," Uncle Calvin hedged. "She definitely thought this up, but you're not trapped in her mind."

"Does that mean I'm really here?"

"Safe in your home? Yes."

"Are you really here?"

"As opposed to what?"

"A dream. A figment of my imagination. A delusion brought on by all of the sugar I ate for dessert."

Uncle Calvin chuckled, a bright smile lighting up his handsome features. While Aunt Tillie was short – barely clearing the five-foot mark – Uncle Calvin was tall. I estimated he was about six-foot-five, with a long and rangy frame. He wore a colorful flannel shirt – red and green, of course – and his dark hair was shot through with silver and gray.

"I'm mostly real," Uncle Calvin clarified. "If someone outside of this reality were to walk into the guesthouse, though, he or she wouldn't see me."

"Is that what this is? Am I in an alternate reality?"

"You're in a reality of your making," Uncle Calvin said. "Have you figured out why yet?"

"No, and Aunt Tillie is really ticking me off on this one," I said. "I thought we were trapped in memories – both good and bad – like before. Of course, you don't remember that, do you?"

"I remember."

"How?"

"Your great-aunt remembers and sometimes – mostly when she's sound asleep – she drops her defenses enough to allow me entrance. I like to share dreams with her. It's the closest I'll get to my version of Heaven for a bit."

He was clearly a romantic soul, which baffled me. "Why did you choose Aunt Tillie?"

Uncle Calvin's chuckle was warm and rich. "Oh, you make me laugh. You remind me of her."

"There's no need to be insulting."

"That wasn't an insult," Uncle Calvin clarified. "You happen to be talking about the woman I love. Watch yourself."

"I'm sorry." I said the words but wasn't sure if I meant them. "It's just … by all accounts, you were a saint. How did a saint get saddled with the ultimate sinner?"

"I was never a saint, and Tillie is no sinner. Don't get me wrong, she sins with impunity. That doesn't mean she's bad."

"I'm sure you'll understand that's hard for me to swallow given my current circumstances," I pointed out. "You said she borrowed you. Why?"

"I believe she's going to be caught up with Clove for a bit. Something didn't go according to plan over there."

"Is Clove in trouble?"

"Not the kind you're worried about," Uncle Calvin answered. "She's simply eating up more of Tillie's time than expected. Everything will be fine, Bay. You must know that Tillie would never truly risk your lives."

"Just our mental health."

"That's another thing entirely," Uncle Calvin agreed. "I was reticent when she tapped me for this one. I wasn't sure it was a good idea. I wasn't convinced your sin was one worth punishing. Tillie thought otherwise and, in the end, I couldn't give up the chance to spend time with you."

"And what did she tap you for?"

"To be your guide."

I tugged on my bottom lip as I considered his words. "Our guide?"

"If you think about it, really give it some hard thought, you'll understand what's happening."

I'd done nothing but think about it for what felt like hours. "Can you give me a hint?"

Uncle Calvin smiled. "I'm not sure that's allowed."

"You're in charge for right now," I reminded him. "That means you get to make the decisions."

"I guess that's fair." Uncle Calvin leaned back in the chair, reclining so he could stretch out his long legs. "Okay, well, here's the thing: Your journey will not be complete until you visit the past, present and future. How's that for a hint?"

It sounded like he was playing something of a game, but things clicked into place. "The past, present and future, huh?"

Uncle Calvin nodded. "Do you understand now?"

"I'm not sure, but I have an idea," I replied. "*A Christmas Carol.* That's my story, right? She plopped us in *A Christmas Carol,* and you're the ghost of Christmas present."

"Very good."

"That doesn't make sense, though," I muttered. "You're dead, so you should be the ghost of Christmas past. She should be the ghost of Christmas present."

"Tillie has never been one for conventions," Uncle Calvin volunteered. "I believe she wanted to be your guide for every leg, but running three stories at once tasked her energy. She needs help, so here I am."

That was interesting. "Are Clove and Thistle in the same kind of story I am?"

"No. I believe Thistle is in a horror story and Clove is ... doing something else entirely."

"Did Aunt Tillie really put Thistle in *Black X-Mas?*"

"I believe Tillie puts her own personal touch on everything she dreams up," Uncle Calvin said. "I'm supposed to send you on your way, but it's nice to get a chance to talk to you. One of the things I hate most about my demise – other than the obvious, of course – is that I never got to meet you girls.

"I loved your mothers as if they were my own, you see," he continued. "For a time they were. When I left, the thing I worried about most was Tillie falling apart. I should've known better. She's too strong to fall apart. That doesn't mean she's oblivious to being hurt."

"Is this your roundabout way of telling me I hurt her feelings when I decided to spend Christmas alone with Landon?"

"I wasn't trying to take a long route to the obvious destination. Christmas has always been important to Tillie. Do you know why?"

I shook my head. I'd never considered asking the question.

"Because Tillie has always believed that Christmas is a time of miracles," Uncle Calvin explained. "Her mother was born on Christmas Day. That made it special from the start."

"I didn't know that."

"It's true. Christmas was always a double celebration in the

Winchester house when Tillie and Ginger were young. Then, later, your mother and Marnie were both born in the month of December. It wasn't quite Christmas, but it added to the festivities.

"All through our marriage, even after Ginger died and left everyone bereft, Tillie went out of her way to make Christmas a big deal," he continued. "Even though I wasn't around to see it, I'm going to guess she did the same for you girls when you were young."

"She did," I confirmed, my mind drifting. "When we wanted snow, she made it snow. When we wanted a specific gift, somehow she always managed to make it happen, even when we were low on money. More than that, though, she made the house come alive with decorations and music."

"And despite all of that, you still wanted to have Christmas away from her?"

I balked. "Believe it or not, I wasn't running away from her when I decided to have a quiet Christmas with Landon. I was trying to start a new tradition with him."

"But it wasn't a tradition we should've considered," Landon called out from the open doorway that led to the bedroom. His eyes were alert, even though his hair was tousled from sleep. I had no idea how long he'd been listening.

"Did we wake you?"

"I wasn't asleep," Landon answered, moving to the couch so he could sit with me. He kept his gaze on Uncle Calvin as he maneuvered, his expression unreadable. "I heard you wake up and thought there was a chance it was all a dream. When you got up to look around, I think I knew it wasn't really a dream, but I held on to the hope anyway.

"Then I heard the knock at the door and knew we were in for another mountain of crap and thought maybe we could get out of it if I pretended to be asleep," he continued. "I tried to ignore you guys talking, but it didn't really work."

"So here you are," Uncle Calvin noted.

"Here I am," Landon confirmed. "Checking in for another dose of flogging."

Uncle Calvin barked out a laugh, genuinely amused. "You made a good choice, Bay. He's a proper match for you."

"I wasn't so sure after seeing his teenage self," I admitted. "Of course, I wasn't exactly a dream as a teenager either. I can't really judge him."

"You can judge," Landon countered. "I was a little jerk. I admit it. I didn't recognize it in myself until I was in college. I couldn't go back, so I made a vow to be a better man moving forward. I don't think I became a real man until I met you, though."

"Aw." I rested my cheek on his shoulder. "That could be the sweetest thing you've ever said to me."

"I mean it." Landon rested his hand on my knee and focused on Uncle Calvin. "So what are we in for next?"

"You seem rather resigned to your fate."

"I'm aware that we can't get out of this mess until Aunt Tillie decides we've earned it," Landon countered. "We can't earn it until we jump through all the hoops. I know the drill. If we really are in *A Christmas Carol* – which boggles the mind, right? – then that means we have to get through Christmas present and Christmas future."

"Ooh, do you think we'll be riding around on hoverboards in the future?"

Landon slid me a sidelong look. "I think that Aunt Tillie is looking forward to that one most because she can really mess with us there. We know what happened in the past, so she can't go too far off the rails. But the future isn't set in stone. That means she can come up with some wickedly terrible things."

That hadn't even occurred to me. "She wouldn't do that."

Landon made an exasperated face. "I love you, sweetie, but you're naïve at times. That's exactly what she has planned for us."

I shifted my probing gaze to Uncle Calvin. "Is that true?"

"I don't know what she has planned. I do know what kind of woman she is. She's loyal ... and strong ... and she has an amazing imagination."

"But?" I prodded.

"But she'll mess with you as soon as she gets a chance," Uncle Calvin replied.

"Oh, geez." I covered my eyes with my hand. "I should've seen that coming."

"We both should've seen it coming," Landon said. "Getting out of the last memory was far too easy. It was painful and I'll never be able to live down that car, but the escape was easy."

"Yeah, we're going to have a talk about that car when we're free of this," I said. "I thought only men obsessed with penis size bought Camaros."

Landon scowled. "I was a teenager. I thought it was cool."

"You were a butthead."

"That, too," Landon conceded, gripping my hand. "We need to let it go, though. We're not focusing on the past any longer. We're focusing on the present."

"Right you are." Uncle Calvin brought his hands down on the chair's armrests. "Are you ready for more family fun?"

"Do we have a choice?" I asked.

"No."

"Then sign us up."

"Great." Uncle Calvin beamed. "Have I mentioned how glad I am to get to spend this time with you?"

He was so earnest I couldn't help but return the smile. "That makes two of us."

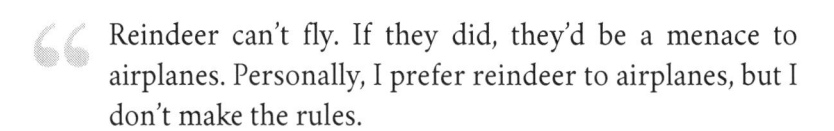

> Reindeer can't fly. If they did, they'd be a menace to airplanes. Personally, I prefer reindeer to airplanes, but I don't make the rules.

— Aunt Tillie explaining how Santa visited the previous night and no one caught sight of the reindeer

NINE

"So, what happens now?"

I expected Uncle Calvin to surround us in magical swirls of light for our jaunt to wherever he planned to take us. If Aunt Tillie was the guide for the past, that meant he was the guide for the present. I was mildly curious who the guide for the future would be, but we obviously had to work our way through this leg before finding out.

"We have several stops to make," Uncle Calvin replied. "I'm actually looking forward to making them."

"Where are we going?" Landon asked, slipping his arm around my waist. "Are we going to visit my parents again? If so, I'd appreciate it if we could refrain from seeing any of my exes."

"We'd both appreciate that," I muttered under my breath.

Landon pressed his lips together, and I could tell he was trying to keep from smiling, but he wasn't entirely successful.

"It's not funny," I challenged, shooting him a look. "You clearly have a type."

Landon's smile slipped. "What do you mean by that?"

"I think she's talking about fiery blondes," Uncle Calvin supplied.

"What? I saw the last adventure. I was waiting to talk to Tillie so I didn't interrupt, but I saw it. You were not a nice boy, Landon."

"Ugh." Landon made an exaggerated face. "I'll never hear the end of this, will I?"

"Probably not," I confirmed. "We're ready, by the way. Take us where we need to go."

"Great." Uncle Calvin's smile was so wide and congenial I knew it was something I'd never forget. I'd seen it in photographs before, of course, but seeing it in real life was something else entirely. "The truck is waiting outside."

I stilled as Uncle Calvin moved toward the front door, confusion etching its way across my brain. "Truck?"

"This isn't the past, Bay," Uncle Calvin said. "It's the present."

"Yes, but I'm guessing that under everything, Landon and I are really still asleep in that room." I pointed for emphasis. "Now you're saying we have to drive to our next location. It doesn't make much sense."

"Who says it has to make sense?" Uncle Calvin threw open the door, allowing a gust of wind and snow to blow inside. I inadvertently shivered as Landon tugged me closer to him. "Life doesn't always make sense, Bay. You of all people should know that."

Resigned, I shuffled toward the door and peered out. "You've got to be kidding me."

"What?" Landon asked, moving to my side. He made a growling noise in the back of his throat when he recognized Aunt Tillie's plow truck. "No way."

"Yes way." Uncle Calvin turned a set of expectant eyes to me. "Let's get to it. You're not the only one I'm excited to see tonight."

"I guess that means we'll be visiting the family," I muttered, reaching for my boots. "How happy will they be to see us?"

"This trip will be different from the last one, Bay," Uncle Calvin said. "You'll see how when we get to our first destination. As for boots … you don't need them." Uncle Calvin snapped his fingers and suddenly my feet were covered with hilariously fluffy witch slippers. "We're behind. We need to get going."

I spared a glance for Landon and found him glaring at his feet, a sparkling pair of new slippers on display. They looked to be bunnies, but it was hard to tell because of the floppy ears and whiskers. "You look cute."

Landon's turn to me was slow and deliberate. "I love you. You know that, right?"

I nodded, biting the inside of my cheek to keep from laughing at the outrage I'm sure bubbled under the surface.

"I think I've more than proven that I'm no longer that cocky kid we saw fighting with his girlfriend – a girlfriend he didn't really care about, mind you – and you should let it go since I'm about to go out into a blizzard with a ghost while wearing ... these." He jerked his foot for emphasis.

I took pity on him. "Did you think I didn't know you were different? I'm hardly the same person I was when I was sixteen either."

"No, but you weren't ... like me."

"You're a boy."

"Thank you for noticing."

"No, I just meant that you were a boy who was active in sports and you were probably popular," I said, shivering as we followed Uncle Calvin into the storm. "You were living a much different life than I did."

Landon helped me into the plow truck, pointing the heat vents in my direction and lifting my hands in front of them so I would be warmed relatively quickly. "You said in the previous memory that our lives weren't all that different," he noted. "Do you still believe that?"

"Yes."

"Even though I was a little bastard to Shelly?"

"I'm guessing Shelly contributed her own brand of drama to that relationship. I don't blame you ... at least not entirely."

"That's a relief." Landon rubbed his hands over mine. "I never realized that she looked so much like you until I saw you standing together."

"She was, like, six inches taller than me."

"Yeah, but the blonde hair and blue eyes ... I must've known what I would like even then." Landon grinned as Uncle Calvin hopped into the driver's seat. "Just for the record, I think this is really weird. I want you to know that."

"Oh, get used to weird, son." Uncle Calvin winked. "You've hitched yourself to this family for the long haul. Things will only get weirder."

"Do you know what happened to Shelly?" I asked, curious despite myself. "Did she ever get over the big heartbreak of ... whatever year that was?"

Landon shrugged as he fastened a seatbelt around my waist – the truck was older so it had a bench seat – and kissed my cheek before reaching for his own seatbelt. "I'm sure she survived the trauma."

"Hold on," Uncle Calvin bellowed, grinning as he put the truck in reverse and floored it, laughing maniacally as he slammed into a snowbank. "Yeehaw!"

Landon widened his eyes to comical proportions. "Oh, geez! You drive like Aunt Tillie."

"Who do you think taught her? Hang on! It's going to be a bumpy ride ... and I mean that quite literally."

BY THE TIME UNCLE CALVIN parked in the Dandridge's parking lot I was feeling a bit sick to my stomach. If we were on a ship, I'd chalk it up to seasickness. We were on land – although close to the lake – and in the middle of a blizzard, so I didn't know what to term it.

"I don't feel so well."

Landon scowled at Uncle Calvin as he helped me from the truck, rubbing his hand over my back as I stared at a snowdrift and seriously considered tossing all the Christmas cookies I ate hours before.

"I can't believe you have such a delicate stomach," Uncle Calvin lamented. "I would've thought Tillie drove that out of you years ago."

"She tried. I'm nowhere near as bad as Clove." Speaking of Clove. I lifted my eyes to the towering lighthouse. "Are we going to see what they're really doing right now or is this more of Aunt Tillie's special magic?"

"I'm not sure what you mean."

"It means that we interacted in memories we shouldn't have been present for during the last leg and it was clear they were hallucinations of sorts," Landon supplied. "Otherwise I think I would've remembered meeting my future self."

"The workings of the witch mind aren't my domain," Uncle Calvin said. "I'm not sure how all of that occurred. You'll have to ask Tillie."

"She's not here, though, right?"

"She's off with your cousin."

"The one we're about to visit," I pointed out.

"Oh, I hadn't put that together." Uncle Calvin tapped his chin as he moved toward the sidewalk, which was completely buried in snow. "I get what you're asking. I'm not sure what we'll be seeing. Perhaps it will be a scene from earlier. It is the middle of the night, after all. Clove is probably sleeping."

"Just like us," I murmured, slipping my hand in Landon's as we moved up the sidewalk. "Every time I think Aunt Tillie can't get weirder – or do something more obnoxious – I'm wrong. She continuously proves me wrong. How is that even possible?"

"She's gifted." Uncle Calvin veered away from the front door when we got to the end of the walkway. "She's always been gifted."

I watched him, a warm feeling filling my chest despite the cold. "You really loved her, didn't you?"

Uncle Calvin nodded. "Of course I did." He looked to Landon. "I'm sure you're wondering why."

"No," Landon replied, taking Uncle Calvin by surprise. "I get it. She was your match. Sometimes things are simply meant to be."

Uncle Calvin pursed his lips. "That makes me feel better about you."

"Were you thinking worse about me?"

"After seeing teenage Landon, who wouldn't?"

Landon scowled. "I'll never get free of that memory, will I?"

I patted his arm. "It's okay. I still have to live with the memory of teenage Bay throwing herself at you. You'll get over it ... eventually."

"That was cute," Landon argued.

"You didn't think it was cute when she said she wanted to keep you."

"That's because she seemed a little oversexed. I couldn't rationalize that version of you with the real you, who is never oversexed."

I scorched him with a dark look. "Did you just call me frigid?"

Landon realized what he said too late to take it back. "Of course not. I ... ." He looked to Uncle Calvin for help. "Do you want to step in here?"

"I think you're doing a hilarious job on your own." Uncle Calvin clapped Landon on the back. "You're a funny guy. I understand what Bay sees in you."

"Oh, geez." Landon pinched the bridge of his nose. "Can we get on with this? I don't understand why we're here."

"You're here to get a picture of the Winchester world," Uncle Calvin supplied. "You're not here to interact with Clove and Sam. You're merely here to see how they spent their evening."

That sounded too simple for Aunt Tillie's deviant mind. "And then what?"

"You'll see ... eventually."

That was far too vague. "I don't like this."

"Welcome to the Winchester world," Landon teased, moving behind me as Uncle Calvin led us to the large window on the Dandridge's main floor. "I don't like this," he said after a beat. "I'm a cop. I shouldn't be peeping through someone's window."

"I promise they're not naked," Uncle Calvin offered. "I wouldn't have taken this job if they were."

"Good to know."

The window was high enough that I struggled to see over the ledge. Landon did his best to help, wrapping his arms around my waist and lifting me. What I found inside was dumbfounding, and not in a bad way for a change.

"They're sitting on the couch drinking hot chocolate and watching *A Christmas Story*," I pointed out, shifting my eyes to Uncle Calvin. "This is hardly earth-shattering."

"I don't believe I said we were going to see something earth-shattering." Uncle Calvin was blasé. "I simply said we were going to see Clove." He kept his eyes focused on her, his lips twitching. "She looks like her mother."

Even though I knew that Uncle Calvin probably wasn't really here – he had to be a manifestation of Aunt Tillie's busy brain, right? – I couldn't help smiling when I realized he was staring at Clove with open adoration.

"Was Marnie your favorite?"

"I didn't have favorites."

"Don't bother lying," I chided. "It's normal to have favorites. Chief Terry taught me that."

"Chief Terry taught you many wonderful things," Uncle Calvin said. "He taught you the same things I taught your mothers."

I'd never looked at it that way, but it made sense. "So, was Marnie your favorite?"

"Your mother was my favorite, but I had a soft spot for all of them, depending on the day," Uncle Calvin replied. "I especially enjoyed watching Twila test every ounce of patience Tillie had. She drove your great-aunt crazy, but she was also the youngest, so Tillie protected her above the others."

"She doesn't do that now."

"Twila is an adult," Uncle Calvin pointed out. "Tillie's protective nature shifted to you and your cousins once the family expanded."

That wasn't exactly the way I remembered it, but now was hardly the time to argue. "What are we supposed to be seeing here?" I asked, turning back to Clove and Sam. They were doing nothing of interest, Sam rubbing Clove's shoulders as she watched the screen and laughed. It was a normal quiet night between the duo.

"Just this," Uncle Calvin said. "You won't understand until we move a bit further into our trip."

"Oh, well, great," I muttered, signaling Landon to lower me to the ground. "This was a waste of a trip."

"No, it wasn't." Uncle Calvin pointed us back toward the truck. "I got to see Clove. She's happy. That can never be a waste."

My heart went out to him. "You're a nice guy, aren't you? Mom always said you were – that you did everything for them when they were younger – but since we never got to meet you it was hard to affix a personality to the photographs. All we know is that you loved Aunt Tillie, and that's hardly a ringing endorsement."

"Oh, you're funny." Uncle Calvin flicked my ear. "It's time to head to Thistle's house. While we drive, you can fill me in on Sam. Do we love him or hate him? Is he good enough for Clove?"

The questions made me bite back a hot retort. He asked out of a place of love. How could I dislike that? "We like him," I replied. "We weren't sure at first, but now we like him. They're getting married soon."

"Tell me about it."

It was a simple request – and I needed something to take my mind off Uncle Calvin's driving – so I did.

"THIS IS A BARN."

Uncle Calvin didn't look thrilled by the sight of Thistle's new home.

"It's a converted barn," Landon corrected, linking his fingers with mine as we trudged through the snow. Even though we could feel the cool breeze and snow whipping by our exposed skin, our feet remained warm in slippers while we hiked through the accumulating snow. "It's actually pretty cool."

"There are two barns here," Uncle Calvin noted, his eyes drifting from one structure to the other. "Why?"

"Marcus owns all of the property," I replied. "He owns the stables over there, although you can't see them because of the snow." I pointed to the east. "He's turning that barn over there into a petting zoo. We get a lot of tourists, so that will be a big draw. He's converting this barn into a house. He's put a ton of work into it. It's really cool."

Uncle Calvin didn't look convinced. "It's still a barn. I don't think I want my great-niece living in a barn."

"It only looks like a barn from the outside," Landon promised. "Trust me. You'll be impressed when you see the inside."

"Besides that, Thistle is the type of person who doesn't like conforming," I added. "Living in a barn makes her feel different and special."

"And Marcus kind of feels the same way," Landon said, leading me toward the front window. "They're a good match. Marcus is calm. Thistle is mean, but has a good heart when she wants to. He reins her in when necessary."

"He also loves her despite – or maybe because of – her flaws," I added. "I thought she would eat him alive for sure when they started dating. Now I'm starting to wonder if he's you."

"Me?" Uncle Calvin's eyebrows flew up his forehead. "Why would he be me?"

"Because Thistle is Aunt Tillie."

"Oh, she won't like it if you say that," Uncle Calvin warned, wagging a finger. "I find it entertaining, though. Let's see what they're doing."

I followed Uncle Calvin to the window, watching his reaction when he first saw the inside of the barn. He let loose with a shaky sigh and wide smile as he absorbed the homey inside of the converted barn. "Oh!"

I nodded. "It has a lot of open space," I supplied. "The ceilings are vaulted so Thistle won't feel penned in. She's the type of person who needs to run free."

"You're Winchesters. You all need to run free." Uncle Calvin smiled as he caught sight of Thistle. She was dressed in a pair of flannel pajamas with feet, the kind you most often saw on kids, and she was laughing as Marcus spun her around the living room floor. "They're dancing."

I followed his gaze, my heart pinching a bit at the sweet sight. "I guess they are."

"It's Christmas," Landon noted. "Everyone should dance on Christmas." He rested his chin on my shoulder as he watched. "We'll find a way to get some dancing in later, huh? I think we'll both need it."

"You'll have plenty of time to dance." Uncle Calvin was wistful as he watched, Thistle's giggles loud enough to wisp through the window. "Never cut short the dancing, son. It's one of the things you'll wish you could go back and do over. It's never good to have regrets. One of my biggest is that I wish I would've danced more."

"I'll keep that in mind." Landon pressed me tight against him. "Is this what we're supposed to see? Thistle dancing?"

"This is just one mile in our journey," Uncle Calvin corrected. "We have others to traverse."

"Great. Where to next?"

"To see the man who I only knew as a boy."

I had no idea what he meant, but I was intrigued. Plus, well, it felt invasive to watch Marcus and Thistle in a private moment. Sure, they weren't doing anything but having fun, but it was still their moment, and we shouldn't have been a part of it. "Lead the way."

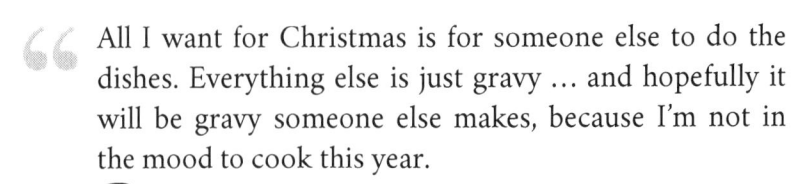

" All I want for Christmas is for someone else to do the dishes. Everything else is just gravy ... and hopefully it will be gravy someone else makes, because I'm not in the mood to cook this year.

—Winnie explaining why she only has one item on her Christmas list

TEN

"Do you know where you're going?"

Uncle Calvin peered through the foggy windshield as he navigated Hemlock Cove's snow-covered streets.

"I do. Just give me a minute to remember. It's been a long time since I've been in these neighborhoods."

"I still don't understand what we're doing," I admitted, holding my hands in front of the heat vents. "We've spent an hour spying on Clove and Thistle in private moments. That seems more invasive than educational."

"I would think you'd have learned by now that your Aunt Tillie isn't one for wasting time on things that aren't important." He uttered the sentence as if it were fact rather than an intriguing and fanciful fiction.

"Really? Last summer she spent two weeks hiding in the bushes by the Crawford farm because she was convinced she was going to catch aliens making crop circles."

Uncle Calvin barked out a laugh. "That sounds just like her."

"I don't see how that was important," I added.

"It was clearly important to her."

"Yes, but … ."

"Oh, Bay, you have a pragmatic streak that skips most Winchesters. I've known quite a few witches over the years, and your mind works differently."

"I happen to like the way her mind works," Landon argued. "I agree with her. I can't see any situation where what we just saw – actually, what we just intruded on – will turn out to be important."

"Give it time."

"I'll add that if Clove and Thistle are being shown private moments from my evening with Bay that's going to make me incredibly uncomfortable," Landon said. "Sometimes things are supposed to be shared by only two people."

Uncle Calvin shifted uncomfortably on his seat. "I'm sure Tillie would never show them your ... um ... private time."

"That's not what I'm talking about," Landon countered. "Some things are private, intimate. I'm not necessarily talking about sex."

"Oh, did you have to use the S-word? You're talking about my great-niece."

"I'm talking about something vague," Landon corrected. "If I find out Aunt Tillie showed anyone else scenes from our night, I'm going to be extremely unhappy."

"I don't think you have to worry about that. Clove and Thistle are on different journeys this evening."

"Whatever." Landon sighed as he collected my hand and held it between his. "This is Terry's neighborhood, isn't it?"

I followed his gaze out the window and nodded. "His house is right around the corner." Something occurred to me. "That's where we're going, isn't it? You said you were going to see a man you knew as a boy. You knew Chief Terry as a boy. You died before he became ... who he is."

"That is where we're going." Uncle Calvin parked in front of Chief Terry's house, his lips curving at the festive lights running along the eave. "He looks like he gets into the Christmas spirit."

"He likes Christmas," I agreed, following Landon out of the truck. "I think he's always been a fan of Christmas. Although ... ." I broke off, remembering the earlier memory. "Maybe he didn't always care about Christmas. He does now, though."

"Why do you think that is?" Uncle Calvin fell into step with us as we crossed to the window.

"You sound like a shrink."

"Perhaps I simply have insight into the witch psyche. Have you ever considered that?"

"Nope." I stopped in front of the window, exhaling heavily as I prepared to look inside. Before that happened, I pinned Uncle Calvin with a serious look. "He doesn't like ... um ... have a lady friend over or something, does he?"

Uncle Calvin chuckled, tickled. "I promise you're not about to have your adoration of Terry blown out of the water."

"I don't adore him," I clarified. "Er, well, I do. It's not that. But he deserves privacy. Aunt Tillie doesn't seem to believe that anyone but herself has earned privacy. That's not the case. Chief Terry deserves his privacy."

"He's alone, Bay."

Something else occurred to me. "That doesn't mean he's not doing something that should be done in private."

"Oh, sick." Landon slapped his hand to his forehead. "Did you have to go there?"

"Not that!" I was scandalized as I shoved my elbow in Landon's stomach. "Don't be gross."

"I'm not the one being gross." Landon ruefully rubbed his stomach. "You went to a scary perverted place."

"I was talking about if he was wandering around in his underwear or something," I snapped. "People do that when they're alone at home. I do."

"You do that when I'm home with you, and I enjoy it." Landon grinned, ignoring the scathing look Uncle Calvin lobbed in his direction. "I'm sorry for thinking you were being perverted, sweetie. I get what you're saying; No one wants to see Terry naked."

I was horrified. "Who said anything about being naked?"

"Oh, you two are just unbelievable," Uncle Calvin muttered. "Do you always argue like this?"

"This is simply the way we communicate," Landon replied. "Sometimes we're soft and sweet. Other times we're clipped and snarky. When we're fighting, we're something else entirely."

"And let's not do that," I suggested. "It's Christmas."

"I have no intention of doing that." Landon ran his hand down the back of my head, as if to reassure me. "I'm nowhere near melting down – at least not yet."

That was good news. I blew out a sigh as I leaned toward the window. "If he's in his underwear I'm totally going to scream and run away."

"Duly noted." Uncle Calvin seemed eager to peer through the window. "Ah. There he is."

I was relieved to find Chief Terry not only dressed, but seemingly involved in some task. He stood next to his dining room table, hands on his hips, and appeared to be talking to himself as he looked at a mountain of supplies.

"What is all that?" I asked.

"I'm not sure," Landon replied. "They look like ... disposable meal trays."

"They do?" I tilted my head to the side, considering. "They do kind of look like meal trays, don't they? I wonder if they're having a special dinner of some sort at the senior center. Although I can't imagine why Chief Terry would be involved."

"Can't you?" The way Uncle Calvin stared at my surrogate father made me question our presence. "I think if you search your heart you'll realize what he's doing."

I glanced at Landon for help, but he was too busy staring at Terry. "Well ... ." I honestly had no idea. "He's clearly preparing meals for some event. But I don't see any food."

"You will."

Uncle Calvin's cryptic responses were starting to get to me. "When? Is some magical Christmas elf going to show up to do the cooking?"

"The cooking is being done elsewhere. Terry is coordinating the effort."

"The effort for what?"

"To help those less fortunate."

I tried to sort through the words. "Do you want to be more specific? I'm honestly lost."

"Terry is a giving soul," Uncle Calvin supplied. "He wants to help those less fortunate. This year he organized a special meal at the senior center. It's open to everyone who needs food and companionship during the holiday, not just seniors."

"Chief Terry did that?" I wanted to be surprised. "Why didn't he mention it? I would've put it in the newspaper."

"Perhaps he didn't want attention."

That sounded like him. I licked my lips, uncertain. "He should've told me. I would've helped him."

"Are you so certain he didn't tell you?"

"Of course he didn't tell me. I listen when he talks."

"Unlike when your mother and aunts talk, right?"

Now he was just being combative. "Why are we here? There has to be a reason."

"We're here to see what the people you love are doing for Christmas. That means we have another stop. Can you guess where that is? I'll give you three guesses."

Uncle Calvin was smug. In all the stories I heard about him over the years he was never smug. This had to be some weird manifestation of Aunt Tillie's twisted brain. "I don't need three guesses," I supplied. "We're going back to the inn. I know we won't get out of our journey through Christmas present without seeing the inn."

"You're very smart." Uncle Calvin smiled. "Come on now. Back to the truck."

I cast another look to Chief Terry, conflicted.

"What's wrong?" Landon asked, waiting for me to join him for the walk back. "You look upset."

"That's because I have a feeling we're about to learn exactly how selfish Aunt Tillie believes us to be."

Landon met my gaze. "Does that mean you don't think we're selfish?"

"No. I wish I could say that. We're definitely selfish. It's just ... if someone had mentioned this charity event I would like to believe we would have donated our time."

"Do you believe that?"

I wasn't so sure. "We were caught up in ourselves."

"We were," Landon agreed. "I don't think he mentioned it to me, though. I would remember that."

I hoped he was right. "Come on. As much fun as it is hanging around with Uncle Calvin, we still have an entire leg of the story to survive after visiting the inn."

UNCLE CALVIN WAS BEYOND reckless when driving to the inn, spinning us into several snow drifts and stopping outside Margaret Little's house long enough to pack the end of her driveway with snow. It was already filled with loose snow thanks to the blizzard, so the mountain of packed white stuff we left behind was something to behold.

Landon's knuckles were white from gripping the door handle when we parked, and my stomach remained twitchy when I planted my feet on the iced driveway.

"What's with the slippers?" I asked as we trudged up the walkway. "Even though it's freezing and I can feel the wind and snow, my feet aren't cold."

"Tillie wants you to suffer, but I think a case of frostbite would be going too far," Uncle Calvin replied, lifting his chin as we approached the inn. "This is so different from when I lived here. None of this was here. Do you remember the house before it became this?"

"Yeah. We've visited a few times thanks to Aunt Tillie's fevered brain."

Uncle Calvin snorted. "Other than that, do you remember it?"

"It's not easy to forget. We grew up here, for the most part. I have more trouble remembering the house I lived in before Dad left."

"But your father is back, right?" Uncle Calvin was legitimately curious. "They're all back."

"They are and we're working to build a better relationship."

"Meaning?"

I shrugged, helpless. "Meaning it's not easy because there are a lot of hurt feelings on all sides. Dad feels like Mom shut him out. Mom feels like Dad abandoned me."

"How do you feel?"

"Caught in the middle because … well … I've always considered Chief Terry to be my father figure. After Dad left, Chief Terry spent a lot of time with us. He took us to the park. He punished us when we were caught doing things we weren't supposed to be doing. He stepped in. I'm closer to him than my own father."

"And you feel guilty about that in some respects," Uncle Calvin surmised. "You shouldn't. Terry gave of himself because you guys needed it. Loving him doesn't mean you don't love your father."

"I know that."

"I knew when your father and mother married it wouldn't work."

The admission surprised me. "How?"

"They were simply too different, which isn't to say that opposites can't make it work," Uncle Calvin replied. "Marcus and Thistle are clearly opposites, but they make it work. It's just … about the time your mother and aunts were getting married gender roles were changing.

"I always knew there was no way to corral Tillie, so I made the decision to love her because she was a free spirit, not despite it," he continued. "As for your father, he loved your mother's wild side, but he was most attracted to her organizational side. She was pragmatic, too."

I scowled. "Are you saying I'm like my mother?"

"I'm saying you're a unique individual, but you have bits of your mother in you."

"I'm not sure that makes me feel any better."

"Ah, the lament of daughters the world over," Uncle Calvin teased, leading us through the front door of the inn.

"What? We get to be inside this time?"

"The kitchen doesn't have any windows."

"Good point."

Uncle Calvin took the time to admire the woodwork – he was something of a carpenter if the stories told about him were to be believed – and by the time we made it to the swinging door that separated the kitchen from the dining room he was excited.

"This place is wonderful."

"It's pretty," I agreed. "It's also comfortable without being ostentatious."

"It's homey," Landon added. "I remember thinking that the first time I walked into this place. I liked it because it felt like a home and not a business."

"Was that before or after you met Bay?"

"After."

"Were you already in love with her?"

"I ... ." Landon broke off, unsure. "I don't know. Sometimes I wonder if I fell in love with her the first time she opened her mouth and insulted me."

"Ha, ha." I poked his side. "That's not how it went."

"No. I guess not," Landon conceded. "Still, I was intrigued by a woman who showed up to cover the opening of a corn maze. I was further intrigued – and completely agitated – by the woman I caught wandering around the same corn maze after dark. By the time you showed up – with your mother and aunts in matching tracksuits, by the way – I was pretty sure I wanted you in my world."

"That's very romantic," Uncle Calvin nodded. "You two are so cute together." He took me by surprise when he grabbed my cheek and gave it a squeeze. "You are going to make it work over the long haul. It's not just because you're right for each other either. It's that Landon here understands that you need to do your own thing. He doesn't try to stifle your creativity while trying to keep you safe. That's always the hardest part to balance."

"I guess you'd know," I said.

"I would, indeed." Uncle Calvin pushed open the door, tilting his head to the side at the sound of voices.

"That's not the right way to do it, Twila," Marnie barked. "You need to make sure the potatoes hold together better so they don't look weird on the plates."

"Where are the plates?" Mom asked. "Terry was supposed to be here ten minutes ago. We can't start doling this stuff out until we have the plates."

"He'll be here," Twila said. "As for the potatoes, it doesn't matter how they look. It matters how they taste. I'm the potato queen. I know when I've made a good potato."

Even though I couldn't see her face, I could practically see Marnie's eye roll. "Oh, whatever. I'm the queen of potatoes. No one has ever tasted my potato salad and said otherwise."

"She's not wrong," Landon said. "That is some freaking good potato salad. I miss it. We had it all of the time during summer and now ... never."

"You'll be excited when she brings it out in time for Mother's Day." I rested my hand on his forearm, thankful he was with me so I wasn't stuck in this nightmare alone. "Mashed potatoes are good, too."

"They are." Landon rested his forehead on mine, briefly giving in to the exhaustion that lined his face. "I'm tired."

"Me, too."

"I'm also sick of seeing things that seem to have no bearing on what's happening," Landon added, lifting his eyes to Uncle Calvin. "Why are we here? We get it. They're going out of their way to put on a charity dinner. We've been so caught up in ourselves – in our first real Christmas together – we overlooked the signs. We're bad people, but we're ready to make up for it. Why are we still being punished?"

"Because you haven't seen everything yet," Uncle Calvin replied. "It's not just knowing that you would have missed out on something important if left to your own devices. There's more."

"What?"

"We're not quite there yet."

"When will we get there?"

"Soon."

"Oh, geez." Landon swept me to him, holding me tight so he could hug the frustration out of his system. "You're lucky I love you. Any other rational man would've run away after the fairy tale world."

"This one isn't as bad," I pointed out.

"No, but it's not good either." Landon planted a hard kiss on my forehead. "We get it. They're cooking dinner and fighting over who's the best cook. That always happens. Where to next?"

"Not far." Uncle Calvin's smile was enigmatic. "In fact, we don't even have to leave this place."

Instinctively I knew exactly where he was taking us. "Aunt Tillie."

"Right again, Bay."

" Thistle just gave me her Christmas list. There are more than one-hundred items on it, and she threw in "world peace" at the end. She said if Santa needs to cut he should start at the bottom.

— Twila studying her daughter's two-page Christmas list

ELEVEN

Uncle Calvin spent a few more minutes watching Mom bicker with her sisters – cackling like a madman whenever an insult flew through the room – before he reluctantly blew them a kiss and pointed us toward the back hallway.

The kiss was sweet, and even though I was agitated the simple gesture hit me like a fist to the stomach.

"You were their Chief Terry."

Uncle Calvin flicked his kind eyes to me. "Your grandfather was gone before they had a chance to remember him. They needed a father figure. The Winchester line is full of women. That doesn't mean men aren't important."

"Has it always been females born to the line?" Landon asked, stepping to the side so I could walk into the hallway ahead of him. "Have they ever had sons?"

"I believe some of the earlier generations had sons. In fact, I think the first all-female generation belonged to Ginger and Tillie."

"And Aunt Willa," I added, making a face. Aunt Willa was technically only a half-sister – and on my great-grandfather's side, so it was hardly important – but she'd felt marginalized her entire life and I didn't want to leave her out of the conversation.

"That's true, but Willa was something else entirely."

"We know the truth. Aunt Tillie let it slip when Aunt Willa and Rosemary visited. They were trying to put a claim in on the property and Aunt Tillie let them have it."

Uncle Calvin was philosophical about the news. "Well, she lasted longer than I thought she would."

"Probably because we only saw them on very rare occasions while growing up. Once, we went to summer camp and Rosemary came. Other than that I can only remember one or two visits."

"You went to summer camp?" Uncle Calvin was intrigued. "How did that go?"

"We pretty much stayed to ourselves. We've never played well with others."

"I went to summer camp a couple of times," Landon noted. "I always liked it. One year we were right next to a girls' camp, and I was totally popular with all the chicks." He realized too late what he'd said and adjusted his tone. "Of course, I'm a better man now and only want to be popular with one chick."

"Very smooth," I muttered, earning a small pinch to my wrist as we wandered through the hallway that led to the family living quarters. "Where did you go to camp?"

"I don't really remember. I think once was in this area, though. I would have to ask my mother."

"It doesn't matter."

"I don't know," Landon countered. "I was thinking maybe we could take a mini-vacation and go camping this summer."

"Where?"

Landon shrugged. "Wherever. I'm not picky. I thought it would be fun to camp out under the stars with you."

"Or we could carry a sleeping bag to the bluff and get drunk in close proximity to a toilet."

"You're zero fun sometimes," Landon complained. "I can't sleep on the bluff. I've seen too many naked women there, and not one of them was you."

Uncle Calvin arched a quizzical eyebrow. "Excuse me?"

"Mom, Marnie, Twila and Aunt Tillie still dance naked under almost every full moon when the weather cooperates," I supplied. "Landon has seen his fair share of ... celebrations."

"Ah." Uncle Calvin chuckled under his breath. "I wondered if that was still going on. From Landon's perspective it must be difficult. From mine it was downright unbearable. I locked myself in the house those nights.

"It's bad enough seeing your future mother-in-law or your girlfriend's aunts," he continued. "Seeing your nieces is criminal."

"I hear that." Landon placed his hand to the small of my back as we emerged in the family living quarters. "What are we doing here?"

"We have one more stop." Uncle Calvin didn't bother hiding his enthusiasm as he moved to the living room, the smile on his face so wide it almost split it in half. He spared little time to scan the room, apparently not caring about the workmanship as much as the woman sitting on the couch watching television. She didn't look in our direction, but Aunt Tillie was animated all the same.

"What is Latin America?" she barked at the television.

"What is Russia?" someone on the television answered.

"Correct."

"Oh, bull," Aunt Tillie muttered, glaring at Alex Trebek. "You're purposely allowing them to answer the questions wrong. That's not fair."

"Oh, good," I muttered, exhaling heavily. "We've watched Mom cook and now we get to hang out with Aunt Tillie while she watches television. What an exciting night."

"I hate to say it, but I'd rather go back to the embarrassing Christmas memory with Shelly Waterman," Landon admitted. "At least that had some action."

"That can be arranged," Aunt Tillie said, shifting her eyes to us. There was a hint of something – devilish delight, perhaps – lurking in the depths of her eyes. "If you want to go back, I can send you there right now."

Landon, realizing the rules had changed, held up his hands in surrender. "I'm good."

"That's what I thought." Aunt Tillie pursed her lips as she turned her attention to Uncle Calvin. "I wondered if you would be getting here soon. I was starting to worry."

"There's nothing to worry about," Uncle Calvin said, leaving Landon and me behind to struggle over the shifting rules of our predicament as he practically skipped to the couch and took his place next to Aunt Tillie. He died young, so he looked like her son rather than husband, but that didn't stop him from excitedly grabbing her hand. "I missed you, my little cookie crumb."

I openly gaped at the endearment. "Cookie crumb?"

"No one is talking to you," Aunt Tillie fired back. "This is a private conversation."

"Then why are we here?" Landon challenged. "Send us back to bed and we'll be out of your hair."

"Unfortunately I don't have much time, so you'll have to stay," Aunt Tillie said. "Now ... sit down and shut up. I'm talking to your uncle."

"Whatever." Landon didn't bother to hide his disdain as he planted himself in the chair at the edge of the room and tumbled me into his lap.

I took advantage of the lull to stare at my slippers, the odd witch faces seemingly staring back. "I'm glad you don't call me names associated with food," I said. "Cookie crumb is a weird nickname."

"I've considered calling you my little bacon slice," Landon teased, rubbing his nose against my cheek. "There would be no higher honor in my world."

"I'm fine with 'sweetie.'"

"You don't want another nickname?"

"You could call me 'your highness' if you're feeling bored."

"I think I'll stick with 'sweetie,' too," Landon said dryly.

"Aren't they adorable?" Uncle Calvin had Aunt Tillie tucked in at his side as he watched us, his face lit with joy. "I'm sorry I missed all of this."

"You missed other stuff, too," Aunt Tillie said. "Like the first time

Clove got her period and became convinced every man in the free world would now try to impregnate her."

Landon furrowed his brow. "What?"

"It's true." I bobbed my head. "We'd been watching *General Hospital* and someone made a joke about how the lead character was a sperm machine and knocked up women just by looking at them. Clove got it in her head that everyone would know she was now a woman. It was a whole big thing."

"I'm glad I missed it."

"Me, too," Uncle Calvin echoed. "I forgot how dramatic teenage girls can be when they grow up in a clump like that."

I decided to be offended on behalf of my gender. "Hey, that's not funny. We don't mean to be dramatic."

"That doesn't mean you're not." Aunt Tillie leaned back so she fit perfectly against Uncle Calvin, the simple movement causing my heart to ache. Yes, she was torturing us on purpose. Yes, she was getting off on messing with our heads. That didn't mean she wasn't tortured herself at times, especially around Christmas when she was without the love of her life.

"Was this whole thing so you could see Uncle Calvin?" I asked, opting to jump on the issue at hand.

"No, and I didn't even think of being able to see him until ... well ... I had technical difficulties."

"With Clove?"

"She's not the only dramatic one," Aunt Tillie replied. "Thistle has been a pain in the keister, too."

"That's probably because you locked her inside *Black X-Mas*."

"I never steal from anyone else," Aunt Tillie clarified. "She is not locked inside *Black X-Mas*. She's locked inside *Blood Red Holidays,* and she's enjoying every minute of her journey."

I had my doubts. "Why did we get different journeys?"

"Because you had different lessons to learn."

That wasn't really an answer. "Where is Clove?"

"She's having fun on her own adventure."

Knowing Clove the way I did, I knew that wasn't true. "Is she freaking out because she's alone?"

"Oh, don't be a kvetch." Aunt Tillie wrinkled her nose. "She's fine."

"That's not what I asked."

"Well, it's the most important thing," Aunt Tillie argued. "She's fine. You're fine. Everybody is fine."

"You know that Thistle is going to go after you for this, right?" I asked, changing tactics. "She won't appreciate being thrown into a horror movie on Christmas Eve."

"Yes, well, I didn't appreciate being abandoned on Christmas Eve," Aunt Tillie pointed out. "I guess we all have our crosses to bear."

"Oh, geez."

Landon put his hand on my hip to quiet me before I launched an all-out verbal war with my great-aunt. "We know we upset you," he said. "That wasn't what we wanted. We thought we wanted to spend Christmas alone because – well, because we were idiots. We realize now that we were wrong."

He was so calm and collected when delivering the statement I almost believed him. Aunt Tillie? Not so much. She blew a wet raspberry and caused Landon's body to tense under mine.

"You're full of it."

Landon gripped my hip tightly as he tried to maintain his temper. "I am not. I am legitimately sorry if we hurt your feelings. That wasn't my intention, and I know it wasn't Bay's either."

"Oh, don't paint me with your special snowflake brush," Aunt Tillie argued. "I wasn't destroyed by your decision. I simply thought it merited more ... examination."

She was talking out of both sides of her mouth, something that agitated me on a normal day. This was pretty far from a normal day. "What do you want?" I asked, working overtime to remain calm even though I wanted to lunge across the room, wrestle her to the floor and poke her until she agreed to send us back to reality. "What are you trying to do with this whole ... thing?"

"I'm honestly not sure," Aunt Tillie admitted. "When I first started, I wanted you to realize you made a mistake. I figured you'd be the easiest because you were starting to waffle before dinner even started.

The only reason you didn't take it back – which would have saved you, by the way – was because Landon wanted a day alone."

"That is not what I said," Landon snapped. "Granted, I suggested a quiet day alone. I thought it's what Bay wanted. If I realized she wasn't happy with the situation, I would've taken it back right away.

"It's Christmas, for crying out loud," he continued. "The thing I want most on Christmas is for Bay to be happy."

"And that's what she wanted for you," Aunt Tillie said. "That's why she didn't back down. Trust me, compared to the other two, you have it easy."

"That really worries me," I muttered.

"They're fine, you big whinebox," Aunt Tillie barked. "There's no reason to work yourself into a twist. Besides, at the rate they're going they'll be finished before you two."

"Why can't we be done now?" I tried to keep the hint of whine from my voice, but failed miserably.

"Because you haven't learned everything I want you to learn yet."

"I told you there was a method to her madness," Uncle Calvin interjected.

"Who are you calling mad?" Aunt Tillie challenged.

"Hey!" I snapped my fingers to pull her attention back to me. "You guys can catch up on your game of 'No, I Love You More' when we're done talking about our problems. We don't want to be trapped on this ride any longer.

"In fact ... um ... we're willing to make a public apology," I continued, briefly wondering if I would regret making the offer. "If you let us out now, we will stand up in front of everyone during breakfast tomorrow – and we will definitely be there for breakfast – and tell them that we were wrong and you were right."

"We'll also tell them that you're unbelievably wise and we don't know why we ever thought about spending the holiday away from you," Landon supplied.

"We'll also donate as much time as necessary to the charity dinner thing you guys have planned at the senior center," I added. "By the way, why didn't you tell us about that? We would've volunteered despite our other plans. Did you think otherwise?"

"No, and Winnie pointed out that you would have done it," Aunt Tillie replied. "The thing is, after the big deal you morons made about your plans during dinner, they felt as if they would have been guilting you into volunteering. They wanted you to do be excited for it, to do it out of the goodness of your own hearts."

"How were we supposed to do it if we didn't know about it?" Landon asked.

"That is a conundrum, isn't it?" Aunt Tillie tapped her chin. "It doesn't really matter. It's clear that you needed a reminder of why Christmas is important to this family."

"No offense, but all we've seen so far is two bad Christmases and two good Christmases," I pointed out. "We didn't need you to teach us a lesson we figured out on our own."

"That's right." Aunt Tillie leaned forward, her eyes gleaming. "You each saw one good Christmas and one bad Christmas from the lives you led before joining together. Why do you think that is?"

"Um ... ." The thought hadn't occurred to me. She was right, though. We witnessed one of each from both of our perspectives.

"Why don't you tell us why that's important?" Landon suggested. "We're exhausted."

"If you don't know, you haven't learned your lesson yet."

"Yeah, it doesn't matter anyway," Landon argued. "You're going to make us go through the whole thing regardless. That's how you do things."

"Besides, the future is the most exciting part, isn't it?" I challenged. "You get to go off script for the future. You were hamstrung by the past – and even a little by the present – but the future is open territory. You can do whatever you want with the future."

"I'm not doing anything." Aunt Tillie adopted an innocent expression. "You're the ones who decide your own future. That's not on me."

She was far too "cat that ate the canary" for my comfort. "This is going to bite, isn't it?"

"Oh, Bay, there's no reason to get yourself riled up. You might find you have some fun checking out the future."

"I know you too well for that."

"And yet ... ." The grandfather clock in the corner struck two. "It's time."

"Time for what?" Landon asked, tightening his arms around me. "Our future isn't going to be in that horror movie, is it?"

"You need to go to sleep to find out," Aunt Tillie replied. "That's what you need to do right now so you can wake up. Did you hear me? Wake up!"

Aunt Tillie bellowed the last word, causing me to struggle to a sitting position in my bed. I was back – again – but the story wasn't over.

"I'm going to kill that old lady when I get my hands on her," I muttered.

"You're not the only one," Landon said. "She's on my list this time. She should be very afraid."

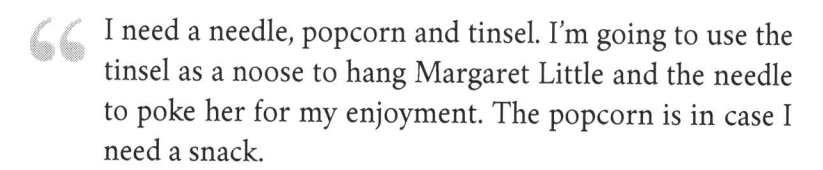

" I need a needle, popcorn and tinsel. I'm going to use the tinsel as a noose to hang Margaret Little and the needle to poke her for my enjoyment. The popcorn is in case I need a snack.

— *A*unt Tillie getting in the Christmas spirit

TWELVE

I immediately tossed off the covers and swiveled my legs so I could climb off the bed. Landon snagged me around the waist before I could escape.

"No." He buried his face in the hollow between my neck and shoulder. "Stay here. Maybe if we're really quiet, really still, she'll forget about us and next time we fall asleep we won't wake up until Christmas morning."

"That's not going to happen."

"I know, but … just give me thirty seconds." Landon sounded so tired I couldn't help but worry.

"I'm sorry about … everything."

"We've talked about this. You don't have to apologize for stuff like this, especially when you didn't cause it."

"My family caused it."

"And I agreed to take them on, too, when I decided I couldn't live without you." Landon pressed a kiss to my neck, his stubble tickling and causing me to giggle. "It's fine. This one isn't nearly as bad as the others. It's almost boring at times."

"Yeah, I can't help but think that's on purpose."

"What do you mean?"

"I mean that she made the memories fairly easy – even the one when you were a teenage reject from *The Outsiders* – and then the present stuff was so boring it was almost mundane," I replied. "All of the stuff from the present was supposed to make us feel like selfish jerkwads."

"I don't want to give that woman more power than she already has, but I do feel like a selfish jerkwad after realizing all the work they put into a party we didn't even know about. When you add to that the fact that it was a party for lonely and needy people, I feel like a tool."

"It wasn't our fault," I protested. "How were we supposed to know that they were planning this? They didn't tell us."

"I hope that's true, but I'd be lying if I said I wasn't worried that someone did tell me and I simply didn't want to hear it," Landon said. "I couldn't see past you. I wanted to make sure we had the best Christmas ever. It was important to me."

"Why?"

"Because we've been through a lot the past year and – while I know that perfection isn't possible – I wanted to make sure you had a great Christmas."

"Really? That's all I wanted for you, too," I admitted. "I wanted to make sure you got everything you wanted."

"I already have what I want. All I care about is spending Christmas with you. If we add the rest of the Winchesters to that mix, it will still be the best Christmas ever."

"Because we're together?"

"That – and I'm sure there will be bacon."

I didn't bother hiding my smile as I hugged him. Hard. Then I remembered what I was going to do before he pulled me back into bed. "I need to go into the other room."

"Why?"

"I need the Christmas book."

"What Christmas book?" Landon's voice was loose, as if he was close to slipping into sleep.

"The one Aunt Tillie wrote," I replied. "It's just like the fairy tale book, but Christmas stories. I think we're stuck in *A Witchmas Carol*. I want to read the story again to see what comes next."

Landon forced his eyes open. "*A Witchmas Carol?*"

I shrugged. "She has a way with titles, huh?"

"Are you saying she wrote her own Christmas book?"

"She likes messing with the written word. She never thinks the original is a good enough story," I explained. "She always figures out a way to enhance it."

"So she did it with Christmas stories and fairy tales. Did she do it with anything else?"

"You don't want to know."

Landon sighed. "Probably not. Where is the book?"

"I saw it on the shelf when I was organizing last week," I replied. "Thistle packed her books, and I thought I was making room for yours until you informed me that you don't own any books."

"Oh, don't say it like that," Landon groused, following me from the bedroom to the living room. "I like to read. I usually do it with magazines, though."

"That makes me a little sad."

"Well, I'll work on that once we're out of this mess," Landon offered. "How does that sound?"

"Divine." I scanned the shelf and grabbed the Christmas book by the spine.

Landon flicked on the overhead light before joining me on the couch. "This is it?" He sent a longing look toward the fireplace. "Do you think we have time?"

"I think it depends on if we're really awake," I answered, flipping open the book. "I'm not convinced we're not sleeping in that bedroom. Aunt Tillie could've easily planted dreams in our heads."

"I thought you told me dream magic was something that witches weren't supposed to dabble in."

"They aren't, but Aunt Tillie fancies herself above the rules. She always has."

"I guess that's true." Landon slipped his arm around my shoulders as he snuggled close and focused on the book. "How much time do you think we have?"

"Not long. Whoever she plans on springing on us for the future show is bound to have meaning ... and probably a sadistic sense of humor."

"That could be any Winchester, right?"

"Pretty much."

Landon exhaled heavily, his weariness dragging him down. "Okay. What do we have here?"

"It's her Christmas book. She took a lot of stories and movies – and even a few very special television episodes – and re-worked them to her liking."

"Like *Little Witches on the Prairie*?" Landon asked dryly.

I smiled at the page he tapped. "She liked *Little House on the Prairie*. The Christmas episodes were particular favorites. On the show, Laura gives away her precious horse to get Ma a stove. In the story Aunt Tillie wrote, her great-nieces sell their services as maids to buy her a new plow."

"Oh, well, that makes perfect sense."

My lips curved as I turned the page. "*Home Alone With Witches*."

"And that is?"

"*Home Alone* ... but with witches. That was always Clove's favorite." Something occurred to me. "Crap! I hope Aunt Tillie didn't shove Clove in that one. She already has a phobia about robbers trying to break in when she's home alone."

"That scenario sounds better than what we're dealing with," Landon argued. "What else?"

"*It's a Wonderful Witch*. *Witch*, which is really *Elf* but about a witch. *A Witchmas Story*, where we all shot each other's eyes out and Aunt Tillie got a whole turkey to herself."

Landon pursed his lips to keep from laughing. "Oh, well ... I feel a bit lucky that we didn't end up in that one. I would hate for you to shoot your eye out."

"It's not funny."

Landon shook his head, solemn. "Of course not."

"It's not."

"I'm not laughing." Landon kept his face even. "What else?"

"Now you're just getting off on the titles."

"Maybe, but ... give me more. I need to know."

"Fine." I flipped through the titles to find the one I wanted. What could it hurt, right? "*Witched*, which is basically *Scrooged*. That one is technically just like this one, but I never realized it. Maybe we're in *Witched* instead of *A Witchmas Carol*."

"Does it really matter?"

"Probably not," I conceded. "We have *The Witchmare Before Christmas*, which she actually tried to film with her own Claymation but lost interest in five minutes after she started. She totally ruined our Play-Doh that day.

"*How Aunt Tillie Stole Christmas*, which really happened, and she added just because she liked telling the story, and *Bad Witch*. Mom was furious when she read that one. It was a recent addition. She always eats pickles when she reads that one."

"Oh, is it any wonder I love this family?" Landon was beside himself with delight. "Tell me more."

"We're running out of time. I need to find *A Witchmas Carol*."

"You can search and talk at the same time."

"Fine." I flipped another page. I'd forgotten some of the titles, so it was nice to be reminded. "*Black Witchmas, The Witchcracker, Miracle on Witch Street*."

"I'm starting to sense a theme here."

"When she finds something she likes, she sticks to it," I acknowledged. "Then there was *White Witchmas, Witch Actually, The Witch Clause* and *Frosty the Snow Witch*. Believe it or not, that last one ultimately turns out to be about a special wine she invented.

"Then there was *Die Witch*, which wasn't really about witches dying but about Aunt Tillie holding off a group of mercenaries in a high-rise building while delivering one-liners like 'Yippee-ki-yah, witch scratcher.'"

"Sounds like a people pleaser."

"It was fairly entertaining," I conceded. "I think *It's a Witchiful Life* was one of my favorites, along with *Witches in Toyland*, which actually turned into a horror movie when Aunt Tillie told us all the dolls looked like clowns and they came alive to stalk the house after everyone went to sleep."

"Ah, well, some traditions live on for a reason."

"Here it is." I found the story I was looking for and began reading. It wasn't that I expected something out of the ordinary – from what I remembered, the story was fairly straightforward – but I wanted to be sure that I didn't miss anything. It took me only a few minutes to skim through it, and when I was finished I found Landon patiently watching me.

"Well?"

"It's the least objectionable of any of her stories," I replied. "In *Home Alone With Witches*, for example, the kid – in this case Clove, because Aunt Tillie was mad at her when she wrote it – is smacked over the head with an empty toy box multiple times before thwarting the robbers. Then, when she manages to do it, she's arrested by the cops because it turns out the robbers were really collectors for a charity and the kid in the story was nothing more than a little witch hole."

Landon couldn't swallow his laughter. "You guys had such a colorful childhood. Even the bad stuff is so hilarious you can't help but enjoy it."

"That's because you weren't around when she read *The Witch-cracker*. Just a hint, the dancing wasn't optional. It was compulsive and unbelievably frightening because none of us have rhythm."

"I don't care what you say. That is funny." Landon touched his finger to the tip of my nose. "She picked this story for a reason. There's nothing funny about it. You said it was the most straightforward one in the book. There has to be a reason she picked that one for us."

"She's punishing us."

"That's the easy answer," Landon countered. "Think. She wants to show us something. She always wants to show us something. Even when she sent us to the really freaky fairy tale world she wanted to show us something."

He wasn't wrong, but still … . "I don't know," I said after a beat. "The stuff from the past is easy. We already did that with her once."

"No, we looked at her memories before," Landon pointed out. "These memories were focused on us. What did they have in common?"

"Mine dealt with my father," I replied. "I was unhappy in the first one and happy in the second. I thought I was unhappy in the second at the time, but it turns out that's one of my favorite Christmas memories."

"Because of Terry," Landon noted. "You were happy because Terry made a fool of himself being Santa and got you the dog you so desperately wanted."

"He did dress up like Santa, but Aunt Tillie secured Sugar," I corrected. "I didn't find out for a few years, but someone let it slip. I think it was Mom. She called Aunt Tillie 'soft' and brought up the dog."

"So Aunt Tillie went out of her way to give you a happy Christmas," Landon mused.

"It wasn't just Sugar. She made it snow that Christmas, too. We were convinced it would be a terrible Christmas without snow and … well … she made it snow."

"I forgot she can control the weather," Landon said. "That still terrifies me."

"What about you?" I asked, shifting my eyes to his. "What did your memories mean? They were shown in reverse order."

"That could've simply been chronological."

"True."

"The first memory, well, I mostly consider that my favorite Christmas even though I was kind of a turd that day," Landon volunteered. "I didn't realize I was having fun until the day was almost over. I remember thinking that I was lucky to have my family that day. I don't know why I remember that part, but I do."

"And the second day?"

"Well ... I wasn't happy that day, but it wasn't for the reasons you might think," Landon said. "It wasn't Shelly. I never felt anything for her, which speaks badly about me because she deserved more, but I didn't care either way about her."

"So why were you unhappy?"

"You saw me. I was a douche."

"Did you have an epiphany that day?"

"Thank you for not arguing with my assessment that I was a douche," Landon muttered. "As for an epiphany, I'm not sure that I ever reached that point. My family was always important to me, but I'm not sure when I got over myself enough to realize that.

"When I was in high school I was kind of a jerk," he continued. "I only cared about being popular."

"With the girls?"

"With everyone."

"Okay, I get that," I said. "I wanted to be popular in high school, too. Lila ran the 'in crowd,' though, so that was never possible for me. I came to accept that at some point."

"I wouldn't have cared if you were popular or not," Landon said. "You know that, right? Somehow, even if I met you then, I would've woken up from my douche dream and become a better man earlier."

"Yeah, you can say that, but we both know it's not true. It's fine. I think we found each other when we were supposed to. That doesn't explain why Aunt Tillie showed us that particular Christmas. There had to be something more to it than forcing me to see one of your girlfriends."

"I don't know why, but I do remember feeling sorry for myself that Christmas," Landon said. "Part of it was Shelly. I thought I was miserable because I was forced to put up with her. In truth, it was because I chose to miss Christmas that day. I didn't realize it until much later in the day, but then I enjoyed a nice dinner with my family."

"So you did kind of have an epiphany," I noted. "You realized you should've been with your family all along. That seems kind of obvious for an Aunt Tillie lesson."

"Yeah, when you add that with the boring scenes of Clove, Sam,

Thistle and Marcus spending time together and everyone else being selfless, it's kind of like a slap upside the head."

"Which means the big lesson will come when the guide for the future shows up," I said.

"I think you're probably right. When do you think that will be?"

I held my hands palms up and shrugged. A split second later the doorbell rang.

"Ask as you shall receive," I said, forcing a smile.

"And here we go again." Landon extended his hand and grabbed mine as we moved to the door. "I'm almost afraid to see who she sent. With our luck, it will be Mrs. Little."

"Probably," I agreed.

The woman standing on the other side of the door wasn't who I expected. Heck, she hadn't even made the list. I was so dumbfounded I could only utter one word.

"Grandma?"

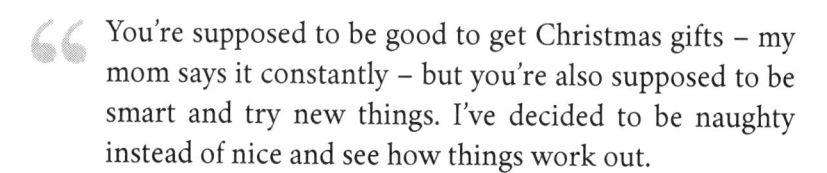

> You're supposed to be good to get Christmas gifts – my mom says it constantly – but you're also supposed to be smart and try new things. I've decided to be naughty instead of nice and see how things work out.
>
> — *Thistle, 11, explaining why being nice at Christmas is overrated*

THIRTEEN

❄

I should've greeted Ginger Winchester with something other than disbelief. I couldn't wrap my head around the situation, though, and I opened my mouth long before I allowed my brain to click on.

"I don't think Aunt Tillie understands how this is supposed to work," I blurted out. "The ghost of the future should be someone who ... well ... is around in the future."

"Bay!" Landon wrinkled his nose.

"Not that I'm not glad to see you, Grandma," I added hurriedly, guilt catching up with me.

My grandmother chuckled. She seemed amused by my reaction. "Well, then, do I warrant a hug?"

"Oh ... sure." I wasn't much of a hugger unless it involved Landon, but I agreeably allowed Grandma entrance and stoically sat back as a ghost hugged me. When she was done, she took a step back and looked me up and down. Her scrutiny made me nervous. "So ... um ... do I pass inspection?"

"You'll do," Grandma replied, taking a moment to study the guesthouse. "This didn't exist when I was still alive. Do you know why they built it?"

"I'm really not sure." Truthfully, I never asked. "It's been here as long as I can remember. In fact, when there was talk of us moving in with Aunt Tillie as kids, I remember Mom, Marnie and Twila arguing about which one of them would get the guesthouse."

Grandma snickered. "Who won?"

"Aunt Tillie. She insisted we all live in the big house, and, as you know, she always wins."

"She does indeed," Grandma confirmed, moving to the fireplace mantel and staring at the photographs there. "This is Clove and Thistle." It wasn't really a question, but I nodded anyway. "You all look like your mothers. It's remarkable."

I stilled, the need to argue with my grandmother's assessment flooding over me. "Oh, well ... I don't think we look that much alike."

"Close enough." Grandma's eyes, which were an odd gray color, didn't move from the photograph. "Clove especially is a mini-version of Marnie."

That I could agree with. "They're built exactly alike," I agreed. "They have the same body types and coloring."

"Which means they're both short and stacked." Grandma's grin reminded me of Twila. "Tell me about yourself, Bay. We don't have much time, but I've always wondered how you girls would turn out."

"Did you ever meet any of them?" Landon took me by surprise when he asked the question.

Grandma shook her head. "I was long gone before any of them came along. That's one of my greatest regrets. I think I would've been a good grandmother. Of course, Tillie was a good grandmother, too."

"I think that's all in how you look at it," I countered. "She was questioned by the police several times while taking care of us. She even went to jail once ... but Chief Terry swooped in and got her out of trouble. Of course, he was the one threatening to lock her up half the time."

"I don't know Terry other than remembering him as a bright-eyed boy with a good heart," Grandma said. "I didn't have an inkling of the sort of man he would become. He's done well by this family, and I know he's loved.

"As for Tillie, while I'm sure her methods were unorthodox – and sometimes even reckless – I'll wager that you remember all the things you did with her during your childhood," she continued. "Were you ever bored with Tillie?"

"No."

"You would've been bored with me at times," Grandma supplied. "I don't say it to be a martyr or feel sorry for myself, but Tillie was always the one with the loud personality. When I died, she was forced to be responsible. Do you know how hard that is when you're the fun one?"

I'd never really considered that. "No. I guess not. It's just ... she's not my favorite person right now. She keeps doing this to us. It's no longer funny."

Grandma chuckled, the sound low and warm as it washed over me. She shuffled to the sitting area to look at the book Landon and I had perused only moments before, grinning when she saw the illustrations. "Tillie always was creative. I never had that going for me. She passed certain creative traits along to your mother and aunts. I'm thankful for that."

"You keep standing up for her," Landon interjected. "You love her."

"Of course I love her. She's my sister." Grandma's eyes flashed as she focused on Landon for the first time. "You're handsome, aren't you?"

"Yes," Landon answered without hesitation, earning a scalding look from me that he ignored. "I've seen photos of you, too. They have quite a few of them up at the inn. You look like a cross between Winnie and Twila. Other than your height, I don't see a lot of Marnie in you."

"Marnie got my body and her father's coloring," Grandma explained. "That somehow made her look like Tillie more than me. Twila got her father's height and my coloring. Winnie got my height – but not the boobs – and my coloring. They're an interesting mix."

"And Bay, Clove and Thistle carried on that tradition," Landon mused. "It's interesting to see them all together. People assume they're sisters, but I think that's more the way they act than the way they look."

"They were raised as sisters."

"I know. The first time I saw Bay with them I thought they were sisters and it weirded me out because I'd never seen siblings as close as them," Landon said. "I love my brothers, but we're not close like these three. I wasn't sure what to make of it."

"And now?"

Landon shrugged. "And now I'm often torn about the mischief they manage to get themselves into," he answered. "Even when they're fighting, they love each other, though. Plus – while I'm not happy about the rules they break and the danger they find – I'm glad that Bay is never alone."

Grandma's gaze turned appraising. "Yes, you'll do." She smiled as she patted his arm before turning back to me. "We still have a lot of ground to cover tonight. Are you ready?"

"If I'm not, does that mean we can be done?"

"No."

I blew out a sigh. I was expecting that answer. "One question before we go," I prodded. "Why would you be the guide showing us the future? You died a long time ago. Shouldn't the guide of the future be someone who will be in the future?"

"I think you're looking at it far too rationally," Grandma said kindly. "Tillie didn't pick guides according to who fit the story. She picked guides because that meant she could have fun with Calvin and me for a time. Christmas was always her favorite time of year, and while this isn't exactly how she'd like things to be, it's a vast improvement over how they are.

"I think she might be a little lonely this year," she added.

I rubbed my cheek as I tried to ignore the guilt flowing through me. "Yes. We're aware. We've already decided to fix it. There's no reason to keep up this charade. We'll spend the entire day groveling in the hope that she forgives us."

Grandma giggled. "You have so much of your mother in you."

"Okay, there's no need to insult me."

Landon quieted me with a shake of his head as he grabbed my hand. "Not that I'm not thrilled to meet you – I've always wondered about you, that's for sure – but do you think we can get moving? I'm tired, and I'm guessing it will take us some time to move through ... wherever you're taking us."

"The future," Grandma offered helpfully.

"Yes, I get we're going to the future, but I've been informed that it probably won't be the real future," Landon pointed out. "Bay says the future isn't set in stone and that time travel is limited to the past for a reason."

I couldn't help but be impressed. "You really do listen when I speak, don't you?"

Landon's grin was sly. "You'd be surprised how often I listen to you – especially when there's no bacon around to distract me." As if on cue, his stomach growled loud enough to fill the room. "At this rate I'm never going to get breakfast."

I patted his arm. "You'll get breakfast. They go all out at the inn for Christmas. Eggs, pancakes, hash browns ... cookies." I was a bit wistful. "We'll be there in a few hours."

"You will indeed," Grandma agreed. "Now, let's get a move on. You've got a lot to see."

I paused by the front door, risking a glance at my pajamas. Grandma hadn't gone through the bother of changing them. "Will this outfit work?"

"Oh, don't worry about that." Grandma beamed. "The place you're going is ... warmer."

Landon shot me a worried look. "She's not sending us to Hell, is she?"

I wanted to scoff at his worry, but I wasn't completely convinced she wouldn't do exactly that to mess with us. "I guess we'll find out."

WE WALKED THROUGH the front door, expecting cold and snow to blanket us, and instead found ourselves in the middle of a sunny summer day. I did a double take, glancing over my shoulder at the guesthouse, but my eyes weren't playing tricks on me.

"I know I'm totally jinxing us by saying this, but I'm already liking the future." Landon held out his arms and lifted his face to the sky, sighing as the sun hit him full on. "I like the seasons – and Michigan in general – but the winter often feels too long. We have two months left. This is nice."

I smiled as I watched him twirl. He reminded me of Clove on spring days when she convinced herself the weather was going to turn early. "It's definitely nice," I agreed. "It makes me think that your idea about camping isn't such a bad one."

"I'm telling you we would have fun camping," Landon said, grabbing my hand. "We wouldn't have to get a tent or anything – although that could be fun – but we could rent a cabin, go fishing, take walks by a river. I think it sounds relaxing."

I wrinkled my nose. "You want to go fishing?"

"You don't have to fish."

"I'll consider it." He was so excited at the prospect I couldn't very well ignore it. If he wanted to camp, we could camp. We simply wouldn't do it alone. We'd take Thistle, Clove, Marcus and Sam with us. The men could fish – or whatever it is men do while camping – and we could sit around the bonfire with cocktails. That's my idea of camping.

"Look at this place," Landon said, shifting gears. "It's the same, and yet it's not quite the same."

I followed his gaze as we passed the bluff, the familiar stones lending an air of comfort even as the trees seemed bigger and somehow ominous. "It does look a little different, huh?" I gripped Landon's hand tighter. "Remember, whatever we see here, it's not necessarily going to happen. Aunt Tillie can't see the future. Even if she was pre-cognitive, which she's not, she couldn't see it in this much depth. That means she's making it up as she goes along."

"I figured that out myself."

"I just don't want you getting worked up over something that probably isn't going to happen," I said. "I mean … think about it. She's trying to punish us. That means she's going to come up with some outlandish scenarios."

"Good point." Landon seemed amiable, the sun doing wonders for his mood. "It'll be okay, Bay. I can guarantee we've been through worse than this."

As if on cue, a couple appeared at the end of the walkway. The woman had long blonde hair cascading down her back in waves – almost to her butt – and the man had short black hair cropped close, and a receding hairline that looked as if it was losing a game of tug-of-war with inevitability. As we closed the distance I realized that we were looking at ourselves ... only from the future. It was surreal and fascinating at the same time.

"We have to hurry," future Bay announced, her gaze weighted as it focused on the other Landon. "Do you have to walk so slowly? You're like a tortoise when you don't want to go to something. We have no choice. We've been over it."

The other Landon, who seemed out of place given the short hair and bored expression, merely heaved a sigh. "I've got it, Bay," he snapped. "You don't have to talk down to me. I hate it when you talk down to me. I'm well aware that we have to go to the old bat's birthday party if we don't want to be cursed. I'm not new."

Once the older couple closed the distance I couldn't help but notice the gray streaking the man's hair and the lines crowding the woman's eyes. They both looked exhausted – and unhappy. I risked a glance at Landon to see if he saw what I did, but he refused to react. He kept a firm hold on my hand and tugged me to the side as the couple strolled past.

The other me slowed her pace, sparing me an odd look as she took a moment to look us up and down. Did she recognize us? Did she understand why we were here? Was she about to impart some great knowledge before telling us to run? She did none of that, instead flashing a bright smile for Grandma's benefit.

"The party will be starting in the garden in about an hour," she offered. "You're early, but I'm sure the lemonade and cookies are already out."

"You had me at cookies," my Landon and the future Landon said at the same time, causing me to widen my eyes.

The other Bay merely scowled at her husband – and the matching wedding rings they wore signified they were indeed married. "I think you've had enough cookies." She patted Landon's stomach. Although he wasn't obese he had put on a few pounds. "I told you twenty years ago that eating the way you do was going to cause issues."

Her Landon scowled. "One cookie won't hurt me."

"That's not what your doctor said," Bay challenged. "He said you need to bring down your cholesterol, eat less sugar and get more exercise."

"I have ideas where I can get more exercise," the other Landon teased, his eyes flashing with flirt.

Bay didn't appear to be interested. "Yeah, you're the reason we have three kids in the first place. Three awful kids. I think we've spent enough time exercising like morons. You can start jogging."

I wasn't a fan of the dismissive way future Bay talked to her Landon, but I was much more focused on the tidbit she dropped about future children. "Three kids?" I mouthed to Landon.

He smirked. "I don't know. I might be able to see that."

"Where are those girls?" Bay asked, glancing around. "We need to get to the guesthouse and change. I told them not to be late."

"They're probably hiding from you," older Landon muttered, not bothering to hide his disdain. "You pick at them so often that's all they want to do."

"Don't you have a slab of bacon to drool over?" Bay challenged dryly.

I moved to pull my hand back from Landon, uncomfortable, but he didn't allow it. He merely shook his head as a trio of teenage girls – a mixture of dark and light hair on their heads – hopped on the trail and headed in the direction of the other Bay and Landon.

"Mom," one of the girls whined, causing me to cringe. She reminded me of Thistle given the dark attitude crowding her pleasing features. "You said you'd wait for us."

Bay shrugged, seemingly unbothered. "You found us. It's no big deal. Now … come on." She snapped her fingers to get the girls to fall in line. "We don't have much time."

"We're not dogs, Mom," one of the other girls complained.

"Of course not." Bay's face reflected distraction. "Now, come on, Sage, Saffron and Sumac. We don't have much time to get ready for the party and I'm already agitated."

"What else is new?" the other Landon grumbled.

I waited until they were out of sight to face Landon. "Okay, I wasn't sure at first, even though I told you this wasn't real, but there's absolutely no way I would name my kids Sage, Saffron and Sumac. This whole thing is bunk."

Landon's eyes sparkled as he tugged me in for a hug. "I figured that out the minute I saw my hair."

" Jingle bells, Mrs. Little smells, Aunt Winnie laid an egg. Aunt Tillie's head is in desperate need of meds, and I'm going to get away ... with everything.

— *T*histle tries her hand at writing a Christmas song

FOURTEEN

"At least the kids were cute," Landon offered, his lips curving. "I knew they would be, but ... ."

"That's what you were worried about?" I was understandably incredulous. "You don't think their names were a bit much?"

Landon shrugged. "I thought Sage was kind of cute."

That was hardly the point. "And Sumac?"

"Maybe we didn't like her. Maybe she was a hard pregnancy or something."

"Oh, whatever." I rolled my eyes and focused on Grandma. She was beyond amused, if her smile was to be believed, that is. "You think this is funny?"

"I think this is just like Tillie," Grandma clarified. "She's clearly given this some thought."

"How far in the future are we supposed to be?"

"You heard the other Bay," Landon replied. "She said we'd been together for twenty years."

"Yes, then she mercilessly picked on your weight."

"Yeah, that wasn't my favorite part." Landon ran his hand over his hair. "Why do you think I cut my hair? Also ... why do you think it was so far back on my head?"

His hair was a point of continual conversation throughout our time together. I understood why it was long when we met. Don't get me wrong, I preferred it long. It gave him a dangerous and sexy vibe that made my heart flutter and toes curl. I don't tell him that, of course, because his ego is big enough. Still, when I picture our future together, he always has long hair.

"Maybe you cut it so you wouldn't look like an aging rocker," I suggested. "There's nothing worse than a hair band member with a bald spot."

Landon narrowed his eyes. "I had a full head of hair. You saw it. I was not bald."

"I'm sorry. I didn't mean to upset you." I patted his hand. "Your hair was a bit thin on top in some places, though. You don't need to dwell on that. It's not real. Everything will be perfectly okay."

"Don't placate me." Landon was back to being grumpy, but he didn't move away from me, instead slipping his arm around my waist. "Don't take this wrong, sweetie, but you were kind of a ... um ... B-word."

I glanced around to see if the kids – correction, our future kids – were back. "Who are you spelling for?"

Landon shrugged. "I have no idea. It just feels wrong to swear knowing that our offspring are running around. Why do you think they're heading back to the guesthouse, by the way? You don't think we still live here, do you?"

That was a sobering thought. "Of course not." I said the words, but I wasn't sure I believed them. I cast a quizzical look in Grandma's direction. "We don't still live in the guesthouse, do we?"

Grandma shrugged. "I'm learning things with you. I have no knowledge of what's going to happen."

"You're not much of a guide," Landon pointed out. "Calvin knew what we were going to see when he took us places."

"That's because even though he was handling this Christmas those things had already happened," Grandma pointed out. "This hasn't happened yet."

"So how does Aunt Tillie know what's going to happen?"

"She ... is very powerful." Grandma averted her eyes. I'd heard stories growing up that she was a terrible liar. She seemed to be proving the stories right.

"Because none of this is going to happen," I corrected. "She made it all up. It's something she imagined for us – while angry, I should point out – so it's going to be absolutely terrible. That's why the other me was so mean to you."

"And why I was fat," Landon added. "What? There's no way I'll get fat."

"I don't want to start a domestic disturbance, but your eating habits are terrible," I pointed out.

"So is your future attitude."

"There's no way I'll ever be that horrible."

"You might, if you decided to emulate Aunt Tillie."

"Oh, that is a terrible thing to say."

"Okay, that's enough of that," Grandma interjected, waving her hands. "We're supposed to head to a party. I think that's what we should do. Starting an argument here seems counterproductive."

I obediently nodded, but didn't miss the challenging look Landon shot me. I knew I should keep my mouth shut, but I'm a Winchester. That means it's essentially impossible for me to do that. "I will never be that mean," I hissed, falling in step with Landon. "I won't care if you get fat because of the bacon."

"Oh, thank you, sweetie," Landon deadpanned. "That makes me feel so much better."

I pursed my lips as I stared at his swinging hand. He didn't automatically reach for me as he usually did. "I'm sorry." I had no idea why I was apologizing. I didn't say it, after all. I still felt guilty. "Don't be angry."

Landon's expression softened. "I'm not angry. I'm just ... tired. I think we should make a pact. We're in this together. Fighting won't do us any good. We need to remember that this isn't real. This is simply something Aunt Tillie dreamed up to mess with us."

"I believe I said that before we left the guesthouse."

"Yeah, you're kind of a know-it-all when you want to be," Landon noted. "Let's try to refrain from saying stuff like that, okay?"

I wanted to argue further, but my attention drifted to the backyard of The Overlook as we crested the final hill. I knew things would change a little, after all, but the sight that greeted me was straight out of a *Star Trek* episode.

"You have got to be kidding me."

Landon snorted, amusement returning. "Oh, now this is more like it."

There was so much going on it was hard to describe – and even harder to latch onto a memory so I could bring it up later when yelling at Aunt Tillie for forcing us through another night of literary hell. The inn looked relatively the same, though I was fairly certain the spinning thing on the back corner of the patio was a transporter of some kind. It made the same noise as the device in Aunt Tillie's favorite *Star Trek* episodes, that's for sure.

The greenhouse had tripled in size and featured a bevy of robots tending to the plants. Yes, robots. They looked like androids from a science fiction movie, but I wasn't sure which one Aunt Tillie plucked them from. Thankfully they didn't wander outside the greenhouse, instead remaining indoors to perform their tasks.

"It's like she has robotic slave labor," I muttered, rubbing the back of my neck.

"She has drones, too," Landon said, pointing to the sky next to the inn. "Do you see those floating things? They're drones."

"I wonder why she thinks she needs them," I mused.

"I'm almost afraid to find out," Landon said. He grabbed my hand as we crossed the lawn, a familiar dark head drawing me toward a picnic table. Even though we were both at risk of losing our tempers, I was determined to do my very best to get out of this unscathed. And, if that wasn't possible, I needed to minimize casualties.

"Clove?"

The woman at the end of the table turned, her expression quizzical as she looked me up and down. I'd recognize her anywhere, the dark hair and upturned nose never changing from when we were kids. The years had been kind to Clove. The look she shot me was not one of friendship, though.

"Do I know you?"

I faltered, unsure how to answer.

"This is Lois and Clark," Grandma volunteered, causing me to grimace as I tried to refrain from groaning at the names.

"Well, at least I'm a superhero this time," Landon murmured.

I squeezed his hand. "Yes, well ... I don't even know what to say about it, so I'm going to pretend it doesn't bother me and hope that I actually start feeling that."

"It's better than Maude."

"I actually prefer the name Maude."

"You're weird."

I poked his side. "You're weird."

Landon smiled, the expression filling me with relief. "It'll be okay," he repeated. It was as if he sensed my worry. "I promise. Don't get all ... freaky ... on me."

"I'll do my best."

"That's all I ask."

Clove, her disdain evident, made an annoyed face. "You must be from the Upper Peninsula contingent. I believe you guys will be seated over there." Clove vaguely waved to a picnic table across the way. She was so superior I wanted to punch her. Of course, she seemingly didn't recognize me, which I was having trouble wrapping my head around.

"Are you here alone?" I asked, glancing around. If I ended up with three kids, odds were that Clove ended up with ten. Aunt Tillie said she was always in love with the idea of being in love. Besides that, Clove was always the most motherly of our little trio. I tended to ignore my dolls, and Thistle occasionally set hers on fire. At least Clove's were always clean and clothed.

"Why do you want to know?" Clove narrowed her brown eyes suspiciously. "Who sent you over here? Was it Thistle?"

No, but I was really hoping she would pop up soon so I could get some answers. "I was just interested."

"Well, I'm not here alone." Clove had an arrogant way of carrying herself, and I didn't miss the way she turned her purse so I could read the "Coach" label while she dug inside. "My husband and daughter are here."

"Oh, really? Where?" Even though I knew it wasn't real, I was mildly curious what Aunt Tillie did to Sam while dreaming up this scenario. He was her least favorite of our beaus – even preferring Landon to him – although she'd come around a bit in recent months.

"There." Clove focused on her reflection as she pointed toward the patio. "He's over there."

"Where?" All I saw was a bald waiter with a tray. "Are you sure?"

Clove ripped her eyes from the mirror, made an impatient noise in the back of her throat and focused on the spot she indicated. "He's right there. Are you blind?"

Agitation bubbled up. "What are you talking about?"

"Um ... Bay." Landon stared at the waiter. "Look closer."

"At what?"

"The waiter."

I did as instructed, frowning when I realized that the waiter – all two hundred and fifty pounds without a stitch of hair – was Sam. "What the ... ?" I turned to Clove, accusatory. "You made Sam act as the waiter?"

"What?" Clove was barely interested in my part of the conversation. She was far too interested in her looks. "He's not the waiter. He's just hungry."

Sure enough, when I risked a glance back at Sam he wasn't delivering the hors d'oeuvres so much as shoveling them into his mouth.

"And you thought I was fat," Landon said.

"I didn't think you were fat. I didn't care anyway. I'll love you no matter what. If you didn't notice, the other Bay was all wrinkled."

"I didn't notice."

I shifted my eyes to him, convinced he was lying. He remained focused on Sam, though. If he was lying, he showed no sign of it. "You didn't notice my wrinkles?"

Landon forced his eyes to me, amused. "No, sweetie. I did notice your hair was really long and you were still really pretty despite how mean you were."

I pursed my lips. "That's kind of sweet."

"Thank you." Landon pressed a kiss to the corner of my mouth. "Now is not the time to disappear into our mutual admiration society. We need to figure out what exactly is going on here. I mean ... Sam is eating his weight in stuffed mushrooms and Clove is ... I have no words for what she is."

He had a point. Clove was ... well ... hmm?

"Horrible," Landon supplied finally, finishing his own thought. "She's horrible. In fact ... ." He didn't get a chance to finish his sentence because our daughters – er, the other Landon and Bay's daughters – made a minor scene as they showed up at the edge of the property.

"Look who's back," I said, pointing.

Landon followed my finger, cringing when he saw they were dressed in matching teal dresses. "I think those dresses are a little skimpy."

"They're also incredibly ugly."

"I can't believe we let them out of the house like that."

I didn't think the dresses were all that skimpy. Ugly? Absolutely. Landon was a new father and being thrown into the deep end right off the bat, so I decided to let it slide. "What kind of party is this?"

Landon shrugged. "I think it's a birthday party. There are balloons."

"Where?"

Landon pointed. "They look like witches."

"That makes sense." I rolled my neck until it cracked, frowning when I saw another girl – this one about five feet tall with brown hair and dark eyes – approaching our girls. "You don't think ... ."

"I see you managed to find dresses at the thrift store, Sage," the girl snarled dismissively.

"Who is that?" Landon asked, flabbergasted.

"It's better than your dress from the short strippers collection at

Macy's," Sage drawled. "How is your job as lead prostitute, Cinnamon?"

I raised my eyebrows, dumbfounded. "Cinnamon?" I risked a glance at Clove. "You named her Cinnamon?"

Clove didn't seem bothered by the potential cat fight on the lawn. "Who are you again?"

"Lois and Clark," Grandma offered helpfully. I'd almost forgotten she was with us.

"Don't you think you should do something to stop that?" I asked, pointing at the girls. "They're about to fight."

"I believe you fought with your cousins when you were that age, didn't you?"

"Yes, but ... it wasn't this sort of fight. In fact ... ."

"You take that back, Sage," Cinnamon snapped. "I am not a prostitute. I hear your mother is, though. Oh, and word on the street is that your father will do almost anything for a slice of bacon, so ... ."

"Hey!" Landon glared at Cinnamon. "Bacon happens to be the best of all the breakfast foods."

Cinnamon rolled her eyes. "You're part of the Upper Peninsula group, right?"

"Absolutely not," I shot back.

"Why do people keep asking us that?" Landon was genuinely curious. "Why do you keep having a negative reaction when they do?"

"Because it's an insult."

"Why?"

"Just ... it is. Trust me."

"Fine." Landon blew out a sigh. "I can already tell I'm going to hate having teenagers, by the way. Just look at the way these girls treat each other. I can't believe you survived this with Thistle and Clove."

I balked. "We didn't talk to each other that way. We fought a bit and there was a lot of dirt eating going on, but we never spoke to one another like that."

"So what's the deal here?"

I held my hands palms up and shrugged. "I have absolutely no idea."

"I won't take it back, no matter what you say," Sage exploded, her fingers lighting with wisps of colored fire as she shot a bolt of magic in Cinnamon's direction. "I hope you get fleas!"

"What the ... ?" Landon moved toward the girl, his face twisted.

"Don't." I grabbed his arm and dragged him back.

"She's going to hurt Cinnamon."

"Wait." I focused on Clove's daughter, cringing when I saw her lift her own fingers, a bit of blue magic kindling. "Oh, crap! This isn't going to be good."

"What?" Landon instinctively covered my head. "What is it?"

"Just ... watch."

"I hope you get chlamydia!" Cinnamon bellowed, whipping the magic at Sage and puffing out her chest in triumph when it smacked the other girl in the chest. "I will make you pay for every terrible thing you've ever done to me."

"Oh, stuff it," Sage shot back. "You're on my list!"

"And mine," Sumac interjected. "You're on my list, too."

Cinnamon made a face. "Oh, no one cares."

"What the heck is this?" Landon was beside himself. "It's like Witch War III out here."

"This is what happens when you don't spend Christmas with your family," a solemn voice said from behind us. I recognized it right away.

"You're in big trouble, Aunt Tillie!" I swiveled, my finger extended, and then did the biggest double take imaginable. "Are you kidding me? You look exactly the same. How is that even possible?"

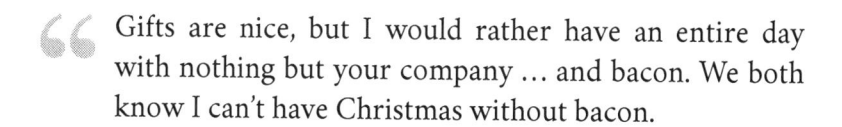

> Gifts are nice, but I would rather have an entire day with nothing but your company ... and bacon. We both know I can't have Christmas without bacon.

— *L*andon getting romantic under the mistletoe

FIFTEEN

"**G**ood afternoon," Aunt Tillie said, her grin evil. She wore a pair of metallic cargo pants with a matching garden hat instead of the hat she usually wore, which had scissors sticking out of it. This one had what looked to be a laser gun firmly affixed to the brim. "Thank you so much for attending my birthday celebration."

"You look exactly the same," I repeated.

"She actually looks younger," Landon commented. "In fact, she looks as if she's aging in reverse."

"That's because I get stronger with age," Aunt Tillie explained. "Soon I'll look better than Bay."

"Hey!"

"You have to admit, the years haven't been all that kind to you," Aunt Tillie noted. "You should've listened to me and embraced your evil side while younger. It's too late to reverse the signs of aging now."

Landon leaned closer. "Is she saying that evil makes you younger?"

I nodded. "Pretty much. She's always told us that."

"Look at me." Aunt Tillie did a little twirl for our benefit. "I clearly know what I'm talking about."

"Oh, whatever." I crossed my arms over my chest.

"I hope you get a club foot!" Sumac screeched in the background. I had no idea who she was cursing, but it was a good bet Cinnamon would be a walking disease factory by the end of the afternoon. "Aren't you going to do something about that?"

Aunt Tillie glanced over her shoulder, blasé. "What would you like me to do? They've been that way since they were little and Sage shoved a pile of dirt into Cinnamon's mouth. That pile just happened to include some worms, which she accidentally swallowed. Then they laid eggs and Cinnamon had to be treated for an invasive worm infestation. It was in all the newspapers because the doctors briefly thought it was some sort of alien invasion. If you ask me, she's right to take her revenge."

Grandma's mouth dropped open. "That is horrible! How did she survive such a trying ordeal?"

I didn't bother to hide my eye roll. "That didn't happen. She's making it up."

"You don't know that it didn't happen," Aunt Tillie challenged. "It did happen. I know. This is the future. Are you from the future? I didn't think so. I'm from the future. I know."

I had my doubts. "I think you're from the present, and the reason you sent Grandma to be our guide is because you have a special role to play in ... whatever it is you have planned here."

"And you're a whiny whiner," Aunt Tillie shot back. "No one cares what you think." She turned her full attention to Grandma. "You look wonderful! I'm so happy to see you."

"You look wonderful, too," Grandma enthused. "I'm so happy to see you!" She threw her arms around Aunt Tillie's neck.

Even though she wasn't much of a hugger – when we were little she was more the pat-on-the-head type – Aunt Tillie returned the hug. "I'm glad you could be a part of this."

I watched them a moment, wonder flowing through me. I always imagined what Aunt Tillie would be like if Grandma survived. I figured she wouldn't be quite so cantankerous, quite so bossy and nowhere near as mean. Still, as great as the moment was, we had other things to deal with.

"Why are we here?" I asked. "What lesson are we supposed to learn from this?"

"You will drown in buckets of blood and an attack of genital warts," Cinnamon screamed, ducking behind a tree as she let loose another bolt of magic.

"Oh, and why do they have the ability to conjure the equivalent of magic grenades to throw at one another?" I added.

"It's the future," Aunt Tillie explained dryly. "Things change when you go into the future."

She sounded as if she was trying to convince herself as well as me. "Fine. Whatever. They're not real anyway."

"You'd like to think that, wouldn't you?"

"There's no way I would ever name my kids Sumac and Saffron."

"Those are lovely names!"

"They're stupid names," Landon corrected. "I kind of like the name Sage, though. It's cute."

I narrowed my eyes. "Don't you think we should focus on the important stuff?"

"I'm just saying that Sage is kind of a cute name," Landon said. "It's ... sweet. The dress she's wearing is indecent, though. I blame the witch influence."

"Oh, whatever." Now he was just trying to be difficult. "Aunt Tillie, we're here. We've played along with your games for hours. Just tell us what you want and we'll do it. We're ready to get out of here."

"And here I thought we were having fun," Grandma pouted.

"Oh, geez." I pinched the bridge of my nose and stared at the sky, tilting my head to the side when I realized I was looking at multiple suns. "Why do we suddenly have two suns?"

"There was an explosion in space ten years ago," Aunt Tillie explained. "Two alien races decided to help, but neither knew the other race was stealing an extra sun from an adjacent galaxy. They both arrived in the nick of time to save us. We didn't want to be ungrateful, so we accepted them both. Now, instead of the Fourth of July we celebrate Twin Suns Day. It's quite the planetary festival."

"Oh, that's not a thing," I complained. "If the sun exploded we'd die right away."

"Are you a scientist?" Aunt Tillie planted her hands on her hips.

"No. Are you?"

"I might as well be one," Aunt Tillie replied. "I watch enough *Star Trek* to know what is and what is not possible. This is totally possible."

"So you are kind of like a scientist," Landon said.

"I could totally do it professionally," Aunt Tillie agreed.

"This is like a hodgepodge of weird stuff that I don't even know how to accept," I muttered, rubbing my forehead. "Aunt Tillie, tell us what you want us to do."

"That's not how this works, and you know it," Aunt Tillie argued. "You have to figure out why you're here on your own."

"But ...."

"Okay, we'll do that." Landon grabbed my hand to quiet me, his eyes moving around the party. When they landed on Sam, I recognized the stirrings of pity – laced with a healthy dose of amusement – in his expression. "Are we here to get Sam's hair back?"

Aunt Tillie followed his gaze, smirking. "Sad, isn't it? He had that full head of luscious hair and then Clove's narcissism knocked it right out of him. It's enough to make a soul weep for the future."

"I thought we were in the future," I challenged.

"No one likes a smart mouth," Aunt Tillie snapped. "As for Sam, life didn't go as he planned. It started out great, of course. He was full of hope and love when he proposed. He thought they'd live happily ever after."

"What happened?" Landon asked, feigning patience.

"They missed Christmas."

"Oh, you have got to be kidding me," Landon hissed. "We get it. We're sorry we were going to miss Christmas. I swear it will never happen again."

"Unless we visit your family," I automatically corrected, cringing when Landon scorched me with a furious look. "What? We can't very well leave your family out of all future plans. It's not fair."

"Fair shmair," Aunt Tillie snapped. "Christmas is mine. Connie can have Arbor Day. No one cares about Arbor Day."

"We'll talk about that later," Landon said, pointedly holding my gaze. "What's important now is that we express how very sorry we are to Aunt Tillie. Not only have we learned our lesson, we're gutted by the idea that we might've ruined Christmas for everyone."

He was laying it on a bit thick for my taste. There was no way Aunt Tillie would fall for that.

"Oh, that's very sweet." Aunt Tillie beamed at Landon, making me think I'd underestimated his powers of persuasion. "But nobody believes that for a second. Quite frankly, you're lucky we're not in a fairy tale world, because you'd be the one with the growing nose this go around."

Landon balked. "I was telling the truth."

"You were full of yourself, and everyone knows it," Aunt Tillie countered. "Ginger, do you think he was full of himself?"

Grandma looked uncomfortable to put on the spot. "I think he's a very handsome boy who seems to love Bay a great deal."

"I don't know how handsome he is, but the love part is right," Aunt Tillie said. "That's the only reason I tolerate him."

"I am extremely handsome," Landon argued.

"Yes, all you're missing is a car-shaped like a penis," Aunt Tillie noted. "You had that when you were a teenager. If I'm not mistaken, you thought you were really handsome then, too."

"I was," Landon said. "I was also a jerk. I try really hard not to be a jerk these days, but it's not always easy because ... well ... I can't seem to help myself from being a jerk when Bay is in trouble. I'm working on it."

"That's not the only time you're a jerk," Aunt Tillie pointed out. "You were a jerk when you ruined Christmas."

"Now you're just playing with me," Landon spat, slapping his hand over his eyes. "You want to see if you can make my head explode."

Speaking of explosions, the bush next to where Clove sat staring at her reflection in the small mirror burst into flames.

"You're going to get warts in places you can't even reach," Sage yelled.

"And you're going to get pregnant in the back of a Volkswagen because you're a total whore," Cinnamon yelled back.

"Hey!" Landon barked, lowering his hand. "No one is a whore! Stop yelling at each other that way. It's not dignified or ladylike."

"Who are you?" Sage asked, sparing Landon a look.

"He's one of the Upper Peninsula relatives," Cinnamon answered. I couldn't see exactly where she was, but she'd managed to find cover in a grove of small trees.

"Oh." Sage wrinkled her nose. "That makes sense."

Landon turned to me. "What is with these Upper Peninsula relatives that I've never heard about?"

"Just think of them as the irregular family members and leave it at that," I suggested.

"We don't like to talk about them because they're kind of like the kissing cousins every family has that no one wants to talk about," Grandma volunteered.

"I don't have kissing cousins," Landon said.

"Don't lie." Aunt Tillie made a tsking sound with her tongue. "It's completely normal."

I shot her a quelling look. "Stop trying to make him uncomfortable. It won't work."

"On the contrary," Landon drawled. "I'm completely uncomfortable."

"See. The boy is learning."

"I hope you look like Aunt Tillie for the rest of your life," Cinnamon screeched from her position in the trees.

"Hey!" Aunt Tillie swiveled and extended a finger. "Do you want to be on my list?"

Cinnamon popped her head up and swallowed hard. "I didn't see you there."

"Obviously not," Aunt Tillie said. "If you feel the need to insult someone by using a family member, who are you supposed to use?"

Cinnamon looked sheepish. "Aunt Thistle."

"There you go." Aunt Tillie turned back to us, all business. "Where were we?"

"Speaking of Thistle, why isn't she here?" I asked, scanning the partygoers. "We haven't seen her yet."

"Don't worry. She'll be along."

"When?"

"Soon."

I narrowed my eyes. "How soon?"

"Very soon." Aunt Tillie averted her gaze. "As for you two, you have a bit of time before you'll be allowed to return home. You haven't yet learned all of the lessons you're meant to learn."

That was the last thing I wanted to hear. "What more do you want us to learn? I've already learned that I will never pick at Landon's eating habits. I will not stick with the terrible child-naming game when it comes to spices. And I will never purposely ruin Christmas again. What more do you want?"

"You'll see." Aunt Tillie smiled as someone called her away from across the lawn. "The president is here. I need to greet him. You guys have a look around. You'll know when you stumble across something important."

Landon furrowed his brow. "What president?"

"The president of the United States," Aunt Tillie replied, offering up a "well, duh" expression as she straightened her hat. "We're good friends. We're such good friends, in fact, that he wanted me to head his security detail. I politely declined."

"Uh-huh." That sounded totally plausible. "And where is he?"

Aunt Tillie pointed toward a figure I recognized from some reality show Aunt Tillie used to watch. I couldn't remember exactly which one, but I knew the face. "He's the president?"

"The aliens didn't like the last one, so we had to replace him."

"Let me guess," I said. "You got to pick the candidates."

"The aliens revere me." Aunt Tillie pasted an innocent look on her face. "I'll be back in a bit. Have fun looking around."

I watched her go with a mixture of amusement and irritation. Aunt Tillie's version of the future was so out there that it was hard to take offense with any of her choices. I firmly believed that – until I saw the massive figure moving across the back lawn. He was so huge he made the runaway troll in the first Harry Potter movie look slim.

"Is that …?"

Landon followed my gaze, his eyes widening to comical proportions when he saw Chief Terry. The man – I was almost certain it was the same man who doted on me whenever he got the chance – looked as if he hadn't said no to many meals throughout the years.

"What happened?"

Grandma moved to my side, her expression unreadable. "I guess that's what happens when you have three women who love to cook fighting over you, huh?"

I shifted a hard look in her direction. "Is that what did this?" Chief Terry had never been what I would call slim, but he'd always been strong and fit. I barely recognized the figure across the way. "Did Mom, Marnie and Twila feed him until … this … happened?"

"He looks like one of those carnival goldfish," Landon mused, tucking a strand of hair behind his ear as he stared at the man he considered to be a friend. "He's one fish flake away from bursting."

I ignored the joke and openly glared. "This can't be right. Even when she's annoyed, Aunt Tillie loves Chief Terry. He stood up for us when we were kids. He took us to the carnival. He dressed up as Santa. He even went to summer camp with us. Oh, and he taught us to fish, too."

I was near tears.

"Bay, it's okay." Landon slid his arm around my waist. "She's making it up. This isn't real."

"I know that." I did. Still … . "The thing is, I always wondered if it could be true. I wanted to ask him why he didn't make a choice, but I always chickened out."

"Why? Because you thought he wouldn't pick your mother?"

"Because I thought he might not pick any of them," I replied. "I want him to be part of our family. I'd be lying if I said that I didn't want him with my mom – although that kind of grosses me out. I can't explain it."

"I get it." Landon pushed a strand of hair from my face. "It's okay."

"I wanted him to be with my mom, to move into the inn and to always be there," I said. "When I was a kid, I always imagined weird stuff like that. It was like a romantic comedy or something."

Landon chuckled. "That sounds fun."

"But then I started wondering about other things," I said. "What if he chose Twila? Then he would be Thistle's dad, and that really irritated me because I assumed he'd switch his favoritism to Thistle."

"I get it."

"The same with Clove. Then it became a thing where I didn't want to risk losing what I already had even if I could win something better."

"Geez. Even as a kid your mind worked overtime, huh?" Landon pressed a kiss to my cheek. "Sweetie, you're an adult now. Terry will always favor you. I think that much is obvious. I think it's okay if he wants to make a choice now.

"Even if he doesn't pick one of your mothers, he'll always pick you," he continued. "Don't get all ... worked up ... over this. I have a feeling this is simply Aunt Tillie's way to force you to have a conversation with Terry while still getting her way on the Christmas stuff."

He had a point. I risked a glance in Chief Terry's direction, frowning when I saw three older witches – women who managed to look older than Aunt Tillie even though they were her nieces – scurry to Terry's side so they could start feeding him with their hands. Marnie actually had grapes, and she popped them off the stems one at a time so she could cater to Chief Terry's rather obvious appetite.

"That is so ... gross."

Landon scowled at the scene. "You're telling me."

"I'm totally going to tell Mom what Aunt Tillie did here. She won't be happy."

"Tattletale." Aunt Tillie popped up behind us, causing me to jolt. "Come on. I'll make introductions. They're excited to meet you."

"Wait ... we're going over there?" That's the last thing I wanted.

"Of course we're going over there. You still have things to learn."

Ugh. This night was seemingly never ending. At least the weather was nice, though.

> Caroling should be outlawed. People act as if strangers coming to your door and singing is a good thing. Let me ask you this, if those carolers showed up during Halloween and had masks and knives, would you think that was a good thing? Singing is just as bad. It's like a knife to the eardrum. I ... what is that? Hot chocolate? You're not giving that to the carolers, are you? How did things go so wrong when I raised you?

— *Aunt Tillie explaining her philosophy on caroling*

SIXTEEN

"Hey, Terry. How's it going?"

Aunt Tillie was all smiles as we approached the table. Mom didn't so much as glance at me – she was too busy feeding Terry a huge turkey leg – but he did a mild double take when he met my gaze.

"Do I know you?"

"I don't think so," I replied haltingly, furious that Aunt Tillie would do something this obnoxious to someone I loved. "I'm pretty sure I'd remember you."

"Of course she'd remember you," Marnie said, flourishing a plate of cookies as she smiled. "I made your favorite: chocolate chip cookies with extra chocolate."

I pressed the heel of my hand to my forehead as I fought to maintain my cool. "Aren't those just normal chocolate chip cookies?"

Marnie spared me a withering look. "Who are you?"

"This is Dwayne and Whitley," Aunt Tillie announced, catching me off guard. "They're from the Upper Peninsula."

"Oh." Mom, Twila and Marnie adopted triple scowls of dislike. "Welcome to the inn."

"Wow," Landon muttered, fighting back the urge to laugh. "I

desperately need to meet these Upper Peninsula Winchesters. If they get this sort of reaction, they must be hilarious."

"Hilarious isn't the word I'd use." I frowned as Twila snatched the plate of cookies away from Chief Terry and handed him a loaf of French bread. "I made your favorite, sugar bear."

How Chief Terry hadn't lapsed into a diabetic coma was beyond me. "Stop that." I grabbed the turkey leg before he could bite in to it, earning a growl for my efforts. "Did you just growl at me?"

"That's my snack," Chief Terry protested.

"You don't need another snack."

"You don't," Landon agreed, grabbing the leg from me. "I, however, am starving."

I watched as he bit into the meat, doing my best to ignore the whining sounds Chief Terry made as he watched Landon devour his snack. "You might want to learn a little something from this situation," I warned, gesturing toward Chief Terry for emphasis.

"What are you getting at?" Landon asked, his mouth full.

"Just that constantly stuffing your face might not be a good idea."

"Hey, I'm not taking anything this world has to offer seriously," Landon said. "We've got kids running around cursing each other, Terry apparently eats his weight in ... whatever he can find ... on a daily basis, Aunt Tillie doesn't age, Sam is bald, Clove is glued to her mirror and for all we know, Thistle is dead."

I stilled. I hadn't wanted to give the fear voice, but I worried about that myself. "Where is Thistle?" I asked, turning my full attention to Aunt Tillie. "You said she would be here."

"She's coming." Aunt Tillie didn't look nearly as bothered by Thistle's absence as I felt. "Don't get your stardust knickers in a twist. By the way, that's actually a thing here. I totally invented it."

"Joy."

"So, Dwayne and Whitley, how long are you staying?" Chief Terry asked, his eyes never moving from the turkey leg Landon gnawed.

"Why Dwayne and Whitley?" I asked, agitated. "I thought we were Lois and Clark."

"I changed my mind. He can never be Superman." She inclined her chin in Landon's direction. "He's far too snarky and broody."

"Does that mean you want me to be Batman?" Landon asked hopefully, tilting the turkey leg in my direction in case I wanted a bite. I forced a smile and shook my head as he happily returned to munching.

"Batman?" Aunt Tillie snorted. "If anyone is Batman, I'm Batman. You can be ... Aquaman."

Landon's smile slipped. "You're on my list."

"Eat your turkey and shut up," Aunt Tillie ordered, focusing on me. "It's a party, Bay. Try to relax."

"I hope you get your mother's butt, Sage," Cinnamon yelled in the background, causing me to hunch my shoulders.

"She's talking about my butt," I pointed out.

"Your butt is fine." Landon patted it for good measure. "You need to chill out. This isn't nearly as bad as we thought it would be."

"Yet," I stressed. "Yet. This is Aunt Tillie we're talking about. Things can always get worse."

"She's not wrong." Aunt Tillie beamed. "Oh, look, the Pope is here."

"The Pope?" She was clearly trying to kill me. There could be no other explanation. When I looked over my shoulder at the man dressed in ornate robes, flowing brown hair offsetting vivid blue eyes, I merely sighed. "He looks like a male model."

"Hey, at least we can say we partied with the Pope." Landon continued working on his turkey leg. "This is good, sweetie. You should try some. You need to keep up your strength."

Speaking of people who were starting to bug me ... . I forced the idea of ripping the turkey leg away from Landon and beating him over the head with it from my mind, instead fixing Twila with a pointed look. "Where is your daughter?"

Twila, who appeared dedicated to feeding Chief Terry bits of bread and cheese, didn't look in my direction. "Oh, Thistle?"

"Do you have any other daughters?"

"No, just the one." Twila was often slow, distracted. Today was no exception. "Why do you ask? Did you hear something?"

I narrowed my eyes. "Tell me about Thistle," I prodded. "How is she these days?" The fact that Aunt Tillie was waiting until the end to unveil Thistle wasn't lost on me. It had to mean something. Thistle often agitated Aunt Tillie most, so I was fairly certain it meant Thistle would get the worst future in Aunt Tillie's little nightmare.

"Do you know Thistle?" Twila asked, confused. "She always told me she'd rather shave her head bald than purposely spend time with the Upper Peninsula relatives."

"We met at a gathering years ago," I lied.

"Oh, well, Thistle is great," Twila enthused. "She's absolutely wonderful. Her husband – well, they're separated, but he's technically still her husband – is a doll, and her children, well, her children could be extras in *The Sound of Music*."

"You're talking about the kids and not the Nazis, right?"

Twila ignored my sarcasm. "I love being a grandmother. Sure, six kids is a bit much, but I wouldn't trade any of them for anything. Er, well, I might trade Fennel for something. But only Fennel!"

My stomach twisted. "Fennel? I am so going to make that woman pay for these names," I muttered under my breath.

"Yes, he looks the most like his father."

"Marcus agreed to let Thistle name his kid Fennel?" Marcus didn't argue with Thistle often, but he held his ground when something was important.

"Marcus?" Twila wrinkled her nose. "Marcus isn't Fennel's father. I mean, sure there was some question about whether Brad or Jim was the boy's father, but Marcus was never in the running."

I widened my eyes as I fought to contain my temper. "I'm sorry ... what?"

"Jim is Fennel's father," Twila supplied.

"Jim who?"

"Jim Patterson."

I racked my brain. "Jim Patterson? The guy who gets drunk and tries to pick up high school girls three times a week?"

"He was Thistle's third husband – and he stopped doing that for a time," Twila said. "I liked her fourth husband much better than Jim, though. And her fifth? I've almost forgotten he's on parole."

"Oh ... my ... ." I couldn't find the appropriate word. When I risked a glance at Landon, I found his shoulders shaking with silent laughter. He kept a firm hold of his turkey leg as he struggled to maintain a calm demeanor. "It's not funny!"

"It's not." Landon fought hard to sober. "It's not funny at all."

"Look at your kid," I ordered, pointing at Sumac as she bent over to grab something from the ground, showing the world her cleavage as she did. "Do you think that's funny?"

"I'm not claiming that kid," Landon said after a beat. "Aunt Tillie is just torturing us."

"Yeah, that's what I thought." I cracked my knuckles as I turned back to Twila. "What happened to Marcus?"

"Marcus?" Twila knit her eyebrows. "Oh, well, he was far too good for Thistle. Aunt Tillie told us that was the case from the start, but we didn't see it."

I slid a hateful look in Grandma's direction. "She's taking this too far."

"I have no idea what you're talking about." Grandma put on an air of faux innocence and light. "I'm just enjoying a beautiful day with a wonderful family."

"Now you're on my list," I warned. "You're nowhere near as sweet and nice as everyone made you out to be."

"That's because Tillie turned me into a martyr after my death. The role never quite fit."

"Oh, whatever." I pinched the bridge of my nose. "Marcus. Where did he end up?"

"Well, after Thistle gave birth to Mace, Marcus thought they should implement some rules for his upbringing," Twila explained. "Thistle wasn't too keen on that. She wanted to raise her children in a bohemian lifestyle because she never found a rule she didn't want to break or a line she didn't want to cross."

I scalded Aunt Tillie with a dirty look. She was busy entertaining the Pope, but she kept staring in our direction to see what was happening. She was having a fine time being queen of the loony bin.

"So they fought about Mace's upbringing? Wait ... Mace is a boy's name. Thistle had a boy?"

Landon lifted his head, intrigued. "She did?"

"All boys," Twila corrected. "Six of them. Sixty fingers. Sixty toes. Six penises. I counted each and every one."

I did my best to keep from exploding. "Yes, well, good for you. So Thistle and Marcus fought over Mace's upbringing," I prodded. "What happened then?"

"Oh, right." Twila broke off another piece of bread and handed it to Chief Terry. "So, they were fighting something fierce – and not having sex – but Thistle turned up pregnant. She claimed it was divine intervention, but Marcus had enough and moved out.

"They tried to make it work for a bit, went to counseling and such, but he walked away not long after," she continued. "He still sees Mace all of the time, but he's king of Hemlock Cove, and his new wife – she was a famous actress, and that chafes Thistle a bit – is queen, and they're very good rulers."

"Hmm. Hemlock Cove has a king and queen?"

"Yes. We love being ruled," Twila confirmed. "Aunt Tillie was queen for a long time – the aliens crowned her – but she decided to step down and let someone else rule. Marcus has been really good at it."

"Well ... awesome," I gritted out, my temper flaring. "So Thistle had another baby ... ."

"Right." Twila nodded. "Dill."

This time I raised both of my hands to my forehead and pressed hard. "Dill?"

"Yeah. He's half gnome. No one talks about it or anything. He's cute, though."

"And his father?"

"I have no idea," Twila replied. "I don't think it matters. Then there's Oregano – he's a real cutie, but dumb as they come. It's okay because we love him anyway. Then, baby Red Pepper Flake brings up the rear."

"Oh, come on!" I slammed my hand on the picnic table, causing Landon to jerk and drop his turkey bone.

"Sweetie, don't let this get to you," Landon admonished, licking his fingers. "It's all made up. None of it's real. Personally, I'm thankful for that. If she gave us something realistic it would haunt us forever. I think she knew that, and even though she wanted to punish us the idea of doing something that might ultimately hurt us was out of the question. That's how we got all of this."

"I hope you get unstoppable gas," Cinnamon bellowed from the other side of the yard. No one so much as looked in her direction, so I figured it must be normal behavior, at least for this whacked-out reality.

"How can you be so calm?" I glared at Chief Terry as he claimed Landon's turkey leg. The meat was almost completely gone, but he gnawed on it all the same. "Stop that!" I extended a finger in his direction. "You're going on a diet. And you three ... ," I broke off and glared at Mom, Twila and Marnie. "You're making things so much worse than they have to be."

"What did I do?" Marnie complained. "I'm just giving my little pudding bear some of his favorite cookies." She made a sound I'd only ever heard women with small infants make.

"Oh, gag me!" I clenched and unclenched my fists before turning back to Twila. "Where does Thistle live now?"

"She lives in a shack out by the Hollow Creek," Twila replied. "Pretty soon it should have running water and everything."

"Oh, that is just ... I can't take one second more of this!" I stormed in Aunt Tillie's direction, pulling up short when I realized Landon wasn't following. I turned back to slap away the cookie he was about to stick into his mouth and murder him with a harsh look. "No more food!"

"Hey, don't tell me what to do," Landon warned. "If you're even thinking of turning into that bossy thing we saw when we first got here I'll have to take a break so I don't strangle you."

I froze, something niggling the back of my brain. "Oh, crap!"

"What?" Landon asked the question while staring longingly at the plate of cookies. "Did you say something, sweetie?"

"Yes." I grabbed Landon's chin and forced him to look at me. "Do you understand what's going on?"

"Yes. You won't let me have a cookie."

"Not that!" It took everything I had not to shake him. "The longer we're here, the more we start to exhibit the traits of the people we saw on the path. You're turning into a glutton, and I'm turning into an absolute shrew."

Even though he was distracted by the cookie, Landon stopped long enough to fix me with a pointed stare. "Do you think?"

"Landon, all you've done is talk about food for the last ten minutes."

"And all you've done is obsess about Thistle and be mean to me," Landon murmured.

"I hardly think I've been mean to you," I protested.

"Think again."

I ran the last few minutes through my head. While I had been forceful with him, I was hardly mean. "You got your turkey leg. You're clearly not suffering."

"There's my mean sweetie." Landon flashed a grin so I knew he was joking and tugged me into his arms. "It's okay. We know it's happening so we can combat it. This is not the end of the world."

The sound of blaring trumpets filled my ears and I leaned around Landon so I could see the side of the lawn. "What's going on?"

"The king is here," Twila enthused, clapping her hands. "He's here and we're all going to get to spend time with him."

"Yay!" Landon brightened. "Marcus is here. He might be able to help us."

"Yes, but Thistle still isn't here, and I'm surprised she hasn't slit her wrists in this reality," I said. "Between Mace, Fennel, Dill, Oregano and Red Pepper Flake – seriously, it's like she just gave up naming kids at some point – Thistle has her hands full. Why isn't she here?"

"Because none of us are really here," Landon replied, craning his neck to see Marcus' entrance. "This is kind of exciting. I never met a king."

"And you're not going to now," I growled. "This entire thing is utterly ridiculous."

"Oh, I don't know. Aliens ... the pope ... the president ... and a king? I don't know why you'd think that's ridiculous."

I mustered a withering look. "I don't want to be mean to you, but you're really starting to get on my nerves."

"Right back at you, sweetie." Landon wiped the corners of his mouth. "Let's get to the king and see if we can get some information. That turkey leg was good, but I'm honestly ready to get home."

He wasn't the only one.

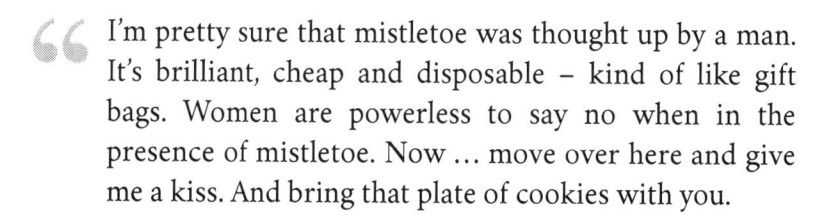

> I'm pretty sure that mistletoe was thought up by a man. It's brilliant, cheap and disposable – kind of like gift bags. Women are powerless to say no when in the presence of mistletoe. Now ... move over here and give me a kiss. And bring that plate of cookies with you.

— *Landon decides to get romantic with Bay*

SEVENTEEN

"Whitley, I'd like you to meet the pope."

Aunt Tillie could have no doubt about why I was approaching her, but she continued the charade.

I spared a glance for the guy to my right, not bothering to hide my eye roll. "You're the pope? Why aren't you at the Vatican?"

"I'm the pope of Hemlock Cove."

"Yeah, because that's a thing," I muttered, grabbing Aunt Tillie's arm. "We need to talk."

"I'm in the middle of something, Whitley." Aunt Tillie dragged out my fake name. "We can catch up with whatever's bothering you at a later time."

"No, I think we're going to catch up now." I forced a smile for the pope's benefit, although much like Chief Terry and Landon, he seemed much more interested in the food than anything I had to say. I dragged Aunt Tillie toward a vacant picnic table, refusing to release my grip. "Marcus is here."

"Oh, really?" Aunt Tillie tipped her head in the direction where Marcus stood with the loyal subjects of Hemlock Cove. He seemed to be having a good time greeting them, even though his crown looked like something he could've picked up at any area Burger King. "Oh, you're right. There he is. Look. Landon – er, I mean Dwayne – is over there with him."

"I see he's married to what looks to be a movie star."

"Yes, Storm."

"Storm?" My eyebrows flew up my forehead. "He married a woman named Storm? What kind of name is that?"

"That was her porn name."

"Now you're just trying to see how far you can push me," I groused, crossing my arms over my chest. "Why would Marcus marry a porn star?"

"Because he's a good man," Aunt Tillie supplied. "Storm didn't want to be a porn star. She had PTSD from her time in the war. He was doing her a favor because he's just that sweet and nice."

"That would be the alien war you saved the world from, right?"

"There was no alien war," Aunt Tillie countered. "The aliens showed up with replacement suns. Get it right."

"Oh, I'm sorry. I have such trouble keeping everything in the future straight because it's like it came out of a fantasy novel."

"Yes, a fantasy novel." Aunt Tillie beamed. "It's funny how things work out, isn't it?"

"Go back to the porn lady. Why would she need to watch porn to get over her PTSD?"

"Not watch it, you ninny." Aunt Tillie made a clucking sound with her tongue, as if she was holding on by a thread because I was somehow the frustrating one. "She filmed it."

"She filmed porn to get over PTSD?"

Aunt Tillie nodded. "There are different types of therapy."

"I so need a drink."

"There's wine over there." Aunt Tillie waved vaguely. "Have as much as you want."

I stared at her for a long moment, emotions I wasn't sure I could identify bubbling up. Finally I adopted a softer tone. "Do you hate us this much?"

Aunt Tillie's shoulders were stiff when she turned to lock gazes with me. "Hate? What makes you think I hate you?"

"Look what you've done," I replied. I don't know if I was hoping to shame her. I was, however, desperate to make her think about her actions. "Clove hasn't stopped staring at her reflection in a mirror. That's not the Clove we know and love."

Aunt Tillie flicked a disinterested look in Clove's direction. "She's always had a bit of a narcissistic side."

"So have you."

"I don't believe you're seeing the world in the manner you're meant to," Aunt Tillie countered. "Perhaps you need to spend more time here."

"Threatening me won't make things better," I argued. "Look at me, for example." I pointed at the unhappy Bay and Landon sitting across the way. "I'm bossing him around, being as mean as possible, and he's eating enough food to put himself in an early grave. Is that how you see us?"

"The boy talks about bacon more than he does sports," Aunt Tillie protested.

"And yet he's risked himself for this family so many times I've lost count," I reminded her. "He's more than just food." I sent a fond look toward my Landon, scowling when I realized he and Marcus were digging into new turkey legs. "Where are those things coming from? He's going to gain ten pounds on this trip."

Aunt Tillie snorted. "Relax. He's fine. You'll both be fine."

"I see what you did here," I supplied, changing course. "You wanted to give us a future to frighten us, but not something that was so bad it sent Landon running for the nearest airport."

"Landon is long past his running days, no matter what I wanted to show him."

I knew she was right, but I was thankful all the same. "Still, you could've made things harder. This is so ... out there ... that all we can do is laugh."

"I don't see you laughing."

"That's because ... that's because I'm stuck in my head right now." I risked a look at Chief Terry. "I think maybe I did him a disservice."

"Oh, geez." Aunt Tillie pinched the bridge of her nose. "You're always such a kvetch. Why are you always such a kvetch? That's Clove's job."

"I'm not sure why I'm a kvetch," I replied. "You showed me this for a reason. Obviously you want me to do something about the Chief Terry situation."

"Bay, I wanted you to be annoyed. That was the most important thing."

"Mission accomplished."

Aunt Tillie preened. "Thank you."

"You wanted to show me something, too," I pressed. "I see it. You wanted me to see Chief Terry this way for a reason. Landon being a glutton is just additional fun for you."

Aunt Tillie flicked her eyes to Landon and Marcus, grinning. "The boy does love his food, doesn't he?"

"Now that he's living so close to the inn I'll have to get him on a workout schedule."

Aunt Tillie snorted. "Don't be a pervert."

"That's not what I'm talking about."

"Close enough."

I rolled my eyes and tugged on my limited patience. "I get what you're trying to do here. We understand that Christmas is important. If it's any consolation, I have a feeling we would've ended up at the inn regardless.

"We would've spent the morning together and then we both would've ended up missing you guys and hiked up there," I continued. "We were never really going to miss Christmas."

"You say that now, but I'm not sure it's true," Aunt Tillie countered. "I know you have every intention of spending Christmas with your family. That's a good thing. You're still not done here."

My frustration, previously burning down to embers, flamed back up. "Why?" I didn't care that a few heads turned in our direction. "Why aren't we done here?"

"Because you have two things left to finish."

I cocked an eyebrow. "Two?"

Aunt Tillie nodded.

"And if we do these two things you'll let us go, right?"

Aunt Tillie nodded a second time. "Your journey isn't quite complete. You'll see the big picture when I'm done."

I wasn't convinced, but I held my palms out in capitulation. "Fine. When will these two things happen?"

"Soon." Aunt Tillie's lips curved. "All you have to do until they happen is enjoy yourself."

"I hope you get a period that never ends," Sumac shrieked, something exploding near the tree line. I'd almost forgotten the kids were still here.

"Great. I'm really looking forward to it."

I CONSIDERED RECLAIMING Landon, but he looked happy with Marcus and his turkey leg, so I left him to his business. My mood was one of irritation, and I didn't want to snap at him for no reason. I knew the environment was affecting us – both of us – but that didn't stop my temper from fraying.

I cut through the trees and pointed myself toward the bluff. The area was quiet, laden with power, and I often missed visiting it during the winter months. I figured I might as well take advantage of the odd dream weather and visit our favorite picnic spot.

I thought I'd be alone. Instead I stumbled across Saffron. She sat focused on a book, her back to one of the large boulders cut into the landscape.

"What are you doing here?"

The girl, a genuine mixture of Landon and me, lifted her eyes in surprise. "I thought I was the only one out here."

"I was just taking a walk," I offered lamely, my eyes drifting to her book as I moved closer. *"Lord of the Rings."*

"Yeah, I just started it." Saffron didn't seem worried about the fact that I was a stranger and she was alone. "I really like it."

"That was one of my favorites when I was younger. I desperately wanted to go on an adventure with Aragorn."

"Why? You had an even better adventure here."

I pursed my lips as I regarded her. She seemed amused by my discomfort, something she probably got from Aunt Tillie. "Yes. It seems like you have nothing but adventures here. You have aliens, popes, kings ... it's almost unbelievable, huh?"

"That's because it's not real." Saffron was so matter of fact I couldn't help but jolt.

"You know this isn't real?"

"I know that this couldn't possibly be real," Saffron replied, closing the book and resting it on the ground. "If you really look – which no one here is doing for obvious reasons – you can detect a shimmer in places." She pointed to a spot at the top of the nearest tree. "See. That's not real."

I followed her finger, biting back a sigh. Leave it to Aunt Tillie to create a sentient delusion. That was the last thing I wanted. "If you know this isn't real, what do you remember of your existence before?"

"There was nothing before."

"But ... ."

"There was nothing before and there won't be anything after," Saffron said. "This isn't real. I don't exist."

"You must be the remaining bit of that old psychology textbook Aunt Tillie found at the library's used book sale last year," I mused. "She was obsessed with that thing for a bit. You're far too self-aware compared to the other delusions hanging around."

"I'm sure it takes a lot of effort to control all of this," Saffron said. "It's a pretty piece of land. That's why I chose it."

"It is a pretty piece of land," I agreed. "This is my favorite spot in the summer."

"So the spot is real?"

"It's the only thing she didn't change. Everything else is slightly tweaked. Not this place, though."

"I'm glad it's real." Saffron's smile reminded me of Landon. "Your time here runs short, doesn't it?"

"Apparently not short enough," I replied. "I'm ready to go home. Aunt Tillie says it's not time. She says she has two things left to show me."

"What do you think they are?" The girl looked to be fifteen, but sounded wise beyond her years.

"I don't know. I'm sure they'll be goofy and designed to make me scream."

"She does like things like that." Saffron's bemused expression – so much like her father in this reality – caused my heart to ache.

"She did a good job on you," I said after a beat. I knew I was talking to someone who didn't exist, yet I couldn't stop myself. "You look like Landon. You have his mannerisms."

"Thankfully I don't have his eating habits."

I grinned despite myself. "You're a good girl. You're the nicest of all the girls I've met."

"Those aren't girls," Saffron pointed out. "They're caricatures. They don't have souls … or feelings … or even manners. Aunt Tillie created them to irritate everyone … and they're good at their jobs."

"If that's true, why did she create you?"

"You'd have to ask her."

"I'm asking you."

Saffron shrugged. "Perhaps she made me as a touchstone of sorts. Perhaps she knew you'd need one thing to look at that didn't make you want to weep for the future."

I didn't bother to hide my smirk. "That was pretty good."

"I do my best."

We lapsed into amiable silence, the sound broken only when I heard footsteps on the path. I shifted and found Landon climbing the small hill as he approached.

"There you are. I was getting worried."

I swallowed hard. "Sorry. I just … wanted to look around."

"Okay." Landon's expression was hard to read as he moved to my side. He ran his hand over my shoulder, as if trying to offer me solace even though he wasn't sure I needed it. "I see you found a friend."

"This is Saffron."

"We met on the path between the guesthouse and inn," Landon said. "It's nice to meet you."

Saffron returned his smile. "It's nice to meet you, too. I'm glad to see you managed to pull yourself away from the turkey leg."

"That makes both of us." Landon let out a groan as he sat next to me. "I think I ate too much."

"Really?" I asked dryly. "What was your first clue?"

"The fact that my pants don't seem to want to stay buttoned."

I chuckled at his lame joke. "I didn't mean to wander away. I only wanted a little bit of time to absorb ... well ... everything."

"I talked to Marcus," Landon volunteered. "He's just as amiable as always. He says that he still loves Thistle and wishes her benevolence and light. He claims she's the reason they're not together."

"I talked to Aunt Tillie. She said we have two things to see before we can leave. Unfortunately, she didn't tell me what those two things are."

Landon's hand was gentle as he tucked a strand of hair behind my ear. "We'll figure it out. We always do."

"You're not like the Bay and Landon here," Saffron noted, taking me by surprise when she spoke. I'd almost forgotten she was present. She was much quieter than her teenage counterparts. "The Bay and Landon here have forgotten why they fell in love. I'm not even sure they remember falling in love.

"Right now, they feel as if they're anchored to one another, but not by anything good," she continued. "You, on the other hand, exude love. Even when you could be melting down and taking things out on one another, you lean on one another instead. It's ... refreshing."

"Oh, wow, you're self-aware." Landon was impressed. "Why are you different from the others?"

"Why are you different from the others?" Saffron challenged.

"Because this whole show is for our benefit," Landon answered. "Aunt Tillie wants to teach us a lesson. She's doing a good job of it. I'm exhausted and want to go home."

"Isn't this your home?"

Landon shrugged. "In some ways. Bay is my home, so whenever I'm with her I'm home. This place is different from where we live, though. Aside from being ridiculous, it's also fairly difficult to see those we love struggling."

"Is your world free of struggle?"

"Of course not. It's just ... different."

"And yet you're strong enough to survive that struggle both here and there," Saffron noted, brushing off the seat of her dress as she stood. "I think you're tired, but you're strong. That will benefit you when you take on your last task."

"Oh, well, that's frightening," Landon muttered, exchanging a quick look with me. "When will that be? We still have to figure out what our second-to-last task is."

"No, you don't." Saffron's smile was back in place. "It was me."

"You?" Landon knit his eyebrows. "What do we need from you?"

"The knowledge that you will always struggle," she replied. "If you stick together, though, the struggle won't be nearly as bad as you think."

"I'm pretty sure we already knew that."

"I'm pretty sure you did, too. But Aunt Tillie likes to make doubly sure her lessons are learned." Saffron tilted her head to the side as she stared back at the party. "You should go now. Your last test is about to arrive."

I followed her gaze, but we were far enough from the party that I couldn't detect a shift in the landscape. "I don't suppose you could tell us what to expect, could you?" I asked hopefully.

Saffron shook her head. "No, but you'll be fine."

"How do you know that?"

"Because not everything here is destined to never come true."

I glanced between Saffron and the party, and when I turned my attention back to the girl she was gone. "Where did she go?"

Landon shrugged. "I don't know. I kind of liked her. She's so much different from the others."

"Yeah." I chewed my bottom lip. "I'm kind of sad she's not real."

"Who knows," Landon said, grabbing my hand as we headed for the path back to the inn. "Maybe she will be real someday."

That was a nice thought, however improbable. "Maybe. We're definitely not naming her Saffron, though."

"Oh, that goes without saying. She's also never wearing a dress like that in real life."

" It's so cute that you guys are out here making snowmen. You're in the Christmas spirit this year. It's so great. I … wait. Why does that snowman have a carrot where his pants should be? You're in a lot of trouble, Thistle!

— Twila encouraging the girls playing outside

EIGHTEEN

"She was kind of worth the trip," Landon commented as we walked. "I liked her."

"She was definitely better than the others."

"Oh, I don't know, I kind of like the idea of our kids screaming 'I hope you get chlamydia' at one another when they're teenagers," Landon said dryly. "It makes me feel all warm and full of paternal pride."

I slid him a sidelong look. We'd talked about kids – in a very abstract way – several times the past few months. He wasn't running scared at the prospect. It was also something better left for the future. The real future, that is.

"It won't be like this. You know that, right?"

"I do know that," Landon confirmed. "For one thing, we'll get to meet them when they're young and sweet, so we'll have no choice but to love them when they turn into monsters."

"When puberty hits?"

"Oh, if I have daughters they're never hitting puberty. That will be a house rule."

"What if there are only daughters?"

"That doesn't bother me."

"Are you sure?"

"I'm sure. Still ... ." Landon pulled up short as he came face to face with a boy – he looked to be about ten or so – who had Thistle's eyes and haircut. "You never know. A boy might be in there somewhere."

He wasn't wrong. Of course, odds were that it would be daughters. As long as he was happy, though, I saw no reason to fret.

I focused on the boy, grinning when I read his shirt. "'The only true way to happiness is the witch way,' huh?"

The boy nodded without hesitation. "My Aunt Tillie taught me that."

"And you are?"

"Fennel."

I heaved out a sigh. "I'm sorry you got stuck with that name."

"It's okay. Everyone calls me Fen. It's not so bad."

"It sounds bad to me."

"That's because you're a kvetch." The boy's grin was impish, and he didn't as much as jolt when the sound of magical bombs dropping in the trees assailed our ears. "It sounds like Cinnamon and Sage are gearing up for another war."

"They've been gearing up for that war for hours," Landon supplied. "They're real pains in the ... butt."

"That's because they didn't spend Christmases with Aunt Tillie," Fennel said knowingly.

I pressed my finger to my eye to stop it from twitching. "Really? Is that why?"

"Yes."

"Who told you that?"

"Aunt Tillie. She's the wisest witch in the land." Fennel was solemn, and the way he puffed out his chest told me he had pride in his great-great-aunt, despite the fact that she had saddled him with such a terrible name.

"I'm surprised you're not wearing a shirt that says that," Landon noted.

"Red Pepper Flake is wearing it today," Fennel said. "He's trying to get on her good side because she's been down on him since he pelted her with water balloons last week. He has five of the top ten spots on her list."

"Oh, well, it's probably wise that he tries to whittle those down," I said. "Did you just get here?"

Fennel bobbed his head. "We were late. Mom couldn't find her shoes, keys or marbles."

Landon snickered, earning a dirty look from me. "What? It's funny. Aunt Tillie took out all of her frustration with Thistle on her, and in an ingenious way."

"Yes, but Thistle isn't around to see it," I pointed out. "She's stuck in *Black X-Mas* somewhere and we'll have to explain all of this to her. If you thought it was war before … ."

"Hey, it wouldn't be Christmas without a fight between Thistle and Aunt Tillie. I'm looking forward to it."

Oddly enough, I was, too. To get to that point, though, we had to work our way through this. I shifted my attention back to Fennel. "Is your mother here?"

"Yeah, she's hiding by the punch bowl." Fennel vaguely nodded to the far side of the lawn. "She's doing her best to avoid the king. They used to be married. She doesn't like to think about it."

"I'm sure she doesn't." Landon ruffled the boy's hair. "I think things are about to get rough, so you might want to take cover."

"What fun would that be?" Fennel challenged. "Trouble is my middle name."

"Oh, well … ."

"No, really. It's really my middle name." Fennel turned earnest. "Mom was tired of picking out names and went with that one when she was drugged in the hospital."

"And that sounds just like her." Landon gave the boy a small wave before continuing our trek. He kept a firm grip on my hand, as if he sensed things were about to go sideways. I was glad for it. I could almost sense the wind shifting as we walked.

"What do you think the big finale will be?" I asked, licking my lips as I scanned the various tables. "There are a lot more people here than when we headed to the bluff."

"There are," Landon agreed. "Whatever it is, I'm sure it'll be big. Perhaps the aliens will return and start another war."

"She claims they only dropped off suns and then went on their merry way."

"Do you believe her?"

"I don't believe any of this, although it did give me a thought," I replied. "In this timeline, I figure Aunt Tillie is really supposed to be one-hundred years old – maybe even older."

"She looks better than the rest of us, so I wouldn't worry about it."

"That's not what I'm getting at," I said. "When we do have kids of our own they won't get to spend as much time with her. She's in her eighties now. She could very well be in her nineties before any members of the next generation show up."

"And it makes you a little sad to think that they won't get to know her," Landon mused, rubbing his thumb over my hand. "I don't know what to tell you, Bay. She's strong, but even she can't live forever."

"I wouldn't say that to her," Grandma interjected, popping up in front of us. "She won't like it at all. She wants to live forever."

"I almost forgot you were here." That was true, and I felt a bit guilty for it. "Where have you been?"

"Looking around. It's not often I get to see my children, grandchildren and great-grandchildren all in the same place. I wanted to take advantage and spend some time with them."

"But they're not real," I pointed out. "This isn't how things will be."

"No, probably not," Grandma conceded. "Still, Tillie created this world, and the representations she drew have basis in the people she knows."

"Really?" I couldn't help being dubious. "Clove doesn't sit and stare at herself in mirrors for hours on end. And Thistle would never cheat on Marcus."

"I don't think that's what Tillie is trying to reflect here," Grandma argued. "It's not Clove looking in a mirror that's important. It's that she's distracted and isolates herself from everyone else."

"Oh." Realization dawned. "Aunt Tillie has been complaining that she doesn't see Clove much now that she lives at the Dandridge."

"Yes, and that bothers Tillie," Grandma said. "Your great-aunt is a bit of a curmudgeon."

"I noticed."

"She also has a good heart, and her greatest trait is that she's loyal above all else."

"Did she force you to say that?" I asked dryly.

Grandma shook her head. "You're missing the point, Bay. I'm really here."

I stilled. "But ... how?"

"It's Christmas. Everyone deserves a gift on Christmas. Calvin and I were Tillie's gifts. We were supposed to spend her dreams with her. Unfortunately – or maybe fortunately, given what's happened – Tillie had plans for the evening and she roped us in to helping."

"So you came to invade Aunt Tillie's dreams and got caught in the mayhem?"

"That's rather simplistic, but yes." Grandma smiled. "This ... world ... isn't meant to be a true reflection of what will come. It's supposed to make you think and avoid the obvious stumbles your life will offer."

"Like me eating all of the time," Landon muttered, putting his hand to his abdomen. "She's always said I was a glutton."

"And me being bossy and shrill," I added. "She always thought I tended to take over."

"And she wouldn't like that tendency because she has it, too, and she doesn't want to share the leadership role," Grandma said. "Believe it or not, this night wasn't all about punishment. It was a gift of sorts."

Oh, now she was just making stuff up as she went along. "It wasn't a gift," I countered. "Sure, there were parts of it that were nice. I loved seeing the Christmas when we got Sugar again. I had fun seeing Landon when he was a kid. I even liked the nice pope and king touches here in the future. The rest of it was definitely punishment."

"Well, I didn't say she was perfect," Grandma muttered, causing me to snort. "The truth is, Tillie is very set in her ways. She does things her way, and that won't ever change. She's kept you alive, hasn't she? She took care of you when you were little. She's also there when you're upset.

"I would never pretend that everything she does is right, but she's blamed for the wrong more often than she's exalted for the right," she continued. "You need to give her a break. She brought you here for a reason. All you need to do is figure out what that reason is."

"We already have," Landon pointed out. "We're sorry about wanting to separate for Christmas. We realize it was a mistake. And, believe it or not, we actually want to spend Christmas with her."

"And that's despite all this," I added, gesturing.

"That's good," Grandma said. "I think that means you're almost there."

"Then what are we waiting for?"

"You'll have to figure that out on your own. Still … ." Grandma took me by surprise when she grabbed my shoulders and pulled me forward for a quick hug. "It was good to spend time with you, girl. You remind me so much of your mother."

"And I was just starting to like you," I muttered, earning a chuckle.

"In case things happen too fast, in case I don't get to see you again, you've turned into a lovely woman," Grandma volunteered. "You're bossy and a tad whiny, but you're loyal and strong like Tillie. I'm glad she did such a good job raising you."

"I think Mom is going to have something to say about Aunt Tillie claiming she raised me," I pointed out.

"She might, but she'd never argue that Tillie had a lot to do with how you turned out," Grandma said. "Tillie didn't raise anyone herself – she always had help – but she did do some magical things with you girls, didn't she?"

I couldn't find fault with her logic. "So where is the big finale?"

"Close. It's time to find your final answers." Grandma released me and smiled. "It won't be as hard as you think. Simply open yourself up to the truth."

"Yeah, I think you mean I need to open myself up to Aunt Tillie's truth," I countered. "That is freaking terrifying."

"You can say that again," Landon mumbled.

I watched Grandma move across the party, her interest laser focused on Twila, Marnie and Mom. Sure, the versions of them Aunt

Tillie came up with for this world were absolutely ludicrous, but that didn't mean Grandma wasn't happy to see them.

"This entire thing is crazy," I noted. "On one hand it's mean and cruel. On the other it's kind of funny. It's so surreal it borders on ridiculous."

"That's the way Aunt Tillie rolls," Landon teased, his eyes focusing on a figure sitting at the last table in the row. "There's Thistle."

"Where?" I jerked my head in that direction, smiling when I caught sight of my missing cousin. Her hair was a muted brown instead of the vibrant colors she wore now and she seemed tired, as if raising five kids had drained her a bit. She still looked like Thistle, though. I hurried in her direction. "There you are. I've been looking for you everywhere."

"Who are you?" Thistle asked, her expression quizzical.

"I'm ... ."

"Dwayne and Whitley," Landon gritted out. "We're cousins from the Upper Peninsula."

Thistle quickly lost interest. "Oh. Well, I'm glad you could make it to the party."

"I am, too. I met your son – um, Fennel – on the other side of the clearing. He seems nice."

"He's trouble. They're all trouble."

"Yes, but ... ."

"Is there a reason you're talking to me?" Thistle might've been beaten down, but her temper was still intact. "I don't know you, and I don't want to know you."

"But ... ." I balked. "Why?"

"Because I'm a bitter woman," Thistle replied, her tone remaining even as she parroted back words I'm sure Aunt Tillie planted in her head. "Ever since I missed my first Christmas with Aunt Tillie my life has been on a never-ending downward spiral. I wish I could take it all back."

"Oh, geez." I slapped my hand to my forehead. "This is getting painful."

"You've got to hand it to her," Landon said. "When she finds a theme she likes, she sticks to it." He leaned over and stole a chicken wing from Thistle's plate. "This looks good."

I ignored his obsession with food and remained focused on Thistle. "That's it? You're sorry you missed Christmas with Aunt Tillie?"

"I am," Thistle confirmed. "She was smart and wise, and I was dumb and mean."

"Yeah, the real Thistle would never say that," I said. "I don't care how many twists and turns her life took, she'd never let Aunt Tillie win."

Thistle ignored me. "My life is but an empty shell since I missed that Christmas. Things floundered in terrible ways, and I've done nothing since but try to think of ways to make it up to Aunt Tillie."

"Is that what she wants?" It made sense, in a very odd way. "Is that what Aunt Tillie wants?" I shifted to scan the party. "Where is she?"

"I hope you get fifty pimples on your butt," Cinnamon screamed, an explosion of magic following. This one was near enough to cause me to jerk closer to Landon.

"Hey! That was too close!"

Cinnamon poked her head out of the bushes. "No one asked you. We're having a war here. Do you mind?"

"I do mind," I shot back. "Why are you having a war?"

"Because Mom, Bay and Thistle missed Christmas with Aunt Tillie and ruined all of our lives," Cinnamon replied. "Now all we have are wars."

"Yeah, I saw that coming," Landon said.

He wasn't the only one. I focused on Thistle, willing her to break out of her dazed state and join me in a fight against the evilest Christmas witch of them all. "There's still time to make up for it," I said. "We can all make up for it. Or, we can just not put up with her crap any longer."

Thistle's expression was morose. "I wish I could take it all back."

"Son of a ... !" My temper took over. "Okay, I get it. I've figured it out. Aunt Tillie!" I bellowed her name, glaring when my impish great-aunt popped into view at my elbow.

"You screeched?"

"Yes, I did," I confirmed, feigning sweetness. "I couldn't find you … what with the magical explosions and all."

"Cinnamon can't help herself," Aunt Tillie said. "A lack of Christmases with me ruined their lives. It's all over for them. This is the best they can do."

"I get it," I snapped. "You were right. We were wrong. The thing is, what you don't seem to understand is that we want to spend Christmas with you. We realized the error of our ways hours ago."

"We really did," Landon agreed. "We're sorry."

Aunt Tillie folded her arms over her chest. "Not good enough."

Not good enough? Oh, I knew what she wanted. I grabbed her shoulder and forced her to look at me. I was getting desperate. I knew it showed, but I didn't care. "Not only are we sorry and regretful, but … um … well … ." I wasn't sure I could say the words I knew she wanted to hear. It was the only way out of here, though, so I needed to suck it up and do it.

"You were right," I blurted out. "You were right, and we were wrong. You're the wisest witch in the land and we didn't realize how selfish we were. We were total losers and we're lucky you still find the strength to love us."

Aunt Tillie's face cracked into a slow grin. "Well, what took you so long? That's all I wanted to hear." She clapped her hands, causing the sky to cloud over and snow to begin rushing down. "It's almost Christmas, Bay. You came to your senses just in time. Now … go to sleep. It will be morning before you know it."

> I don't see why men make such a big deal about buying gifts. I'm easy to buy for. I like things that sparkle and smell nice. How hard can it possibly be?

— Thistle annoyed by male shopping habits

NINETEEN

I rolled to a sitting position in the bed, my eyes busy as they scanned the right and left sides of the room. We were alone, back where we started, and it was still dark outside.

"Landon?"

He was beside me, but he didn't bolt upright. He merely stared at the ceiling. I took a moment to let my eyes adjust and then rested my hand on his shoulder.

"Landon?"

"I'm here, sweetie." Landon gathered my hand and pressed a kiss to the palm. "I'm just ... thinking."

"About the pope?"

Landon snickered. "About everything. It looks like you were right. We were here dreaming the entire time."

"Did you doubt that? Grandma basically told us that outright."

"When?"

"She said that she and Uncle Calvin were visiting Aunt Tillie in her dreams for Christmas," I reminded him. "She had other plans when they got there, but they were always in our dreams."

"Well, I don't think it really matters," Landon noted. "We're here, and it's over." He rolled to face me. "It's over, right?"

That was a good question. I looked at the clock, focusing on the muted electronic digits. "It's almost four."

"Which means we still have a few hours to sleep," Landon noted, grabbing my arm to tug me down. He tucked me in at his side and pressed a kiss to my forehead. "Do you hear the wind? It's still roaring. It's supposed to stop at six, though."

"And then what?" I nestled my head on his shoulder. "What are we going to do?"

"Spend time with the family. It's Christmas, after all."

"We need to call Clove and Thistle when we wake up, make sure they're coming, too. It won't be Christmas without them."

"Don't worry, Bay. We'll have a great Christmas."

"I bet you'll even get bacon," I teased, poking his stomach.

"Don't do that," Landon warned, taking on a grumpy tone. "My stomach is upset. I think I ate too much turkey."

I arched an eyebrow surprised. "We were in a dream. You didn't eat anything."

"I still have indigestion." Landon shifted. "Rub my belly."

Another gift from Aunt Tillie. It really was the holiday season.

"THIS ABSOLUTELY BITES."

Three hours later, Landon and I were showered and changed. Once we opened the front door, though, we found ourselves snowed in. We had more than a foot of fresh powder. That meant we had to shovel if we expected to get Landon's Ford Explorer out of the driveway.

"What do you want me to do?" I challenged, my nose and cheeks bitterly cold. "I'm moving as fast as I can. If you ask me, shoveling is men's work."

"How incredibly sexist." Landon planted a kiss on the tip of my nose. He'd bounced back from his stomachache remarkably quickly and was now practically panting at the idea of breakfast at the inn. To make that happen, we needed to get out of the driveway.

"Come on, Bay. Put your back in to it." Landon shot me a pointed look before moving to a spot behind the Explorer. "You're supposed to be tough. You're supposed to believe that women can do the same work as men... only better."

I opened my stance and bent over, scooping a huge mound of snow – before lobbing it at Landon. It hit him square in the face, causing me to giggle as he glared while wiping it away.

"That was very immature."

"I stand by my earlier statement," I said. "I think men should have to shovel."

"And what should women have to do? Knit?"

I shook my head. "The only thing knitting needles are good for is stabbing people."

"Okay, well... what should women do?"

"We give birth. Isn't that enough?"

Landon snorted, genuinely amused. "You have a point."

"Does that mean I'm done shoveling?"

"No."

I pushed out my bottom lip. "Come on, Landon. I gave birth to three children for you and two of them were terrible human beings. I think I've done my part."

"That did it." Landon was already moving toward me. He tackled me into the nearby snowdrift, causing me to squeal as he shoveled snow on my face. "Don't even think of using that against me ever again," he ordered. "Those children weren't real."

"And I'm thankful for that." I grew silent for a moment. "Although, Saffron wasn't bad. I know she wasn't real and was meant to give us a specific message, but I saw a lot of you in her."

Landon tilted his head to the side, considering. "She wasn't real. That doesn't mean we'll forget her. She said some wise things. That proves she was my daughter."

"Oh, you suck." I rolled in the snow with him, laughing so hard my lungs hurt from the cold. The blizzard gave way to a beautiful day – other than all the fresh snow, of course. The sun shined, causing the snow to glisten, and even though I was freezing despite my heavy winter coat, the moment was warm.

"Merry Christmas, sweetie," Landon whispered right before pressing a long kiss to my mouth. I was breathless when we separated. "Now get up and get to work." He tossed a bit more snow on me before standing, turning his attention to the road when a familiar truck stopped at the end of the driveway. "It's Marcus."

I followed his gaze, grinning when I saw Thistle hop out, shovel in her hand and a huge smile on her face. "What are you doing here?" I called out.

"We're here for Christmas," Thistle replied. "Marcus has a snow blower at home so it wasn't hard to dig ourselves out. Sam and Clove are on their way, too. They were just finishing up their cleanup efforts. We figured you might need some help."

I took a moment to study her as she closed the distance. Her cheeks were flushed from the cold, but she looked none the worse for wear otherwise. "How was your night?"

Thistle pursed her lips. "Long. How was yours?"

"Long."

"Even though I'm thankful to be out of it – and I truly am – I'm going to make that old woman pay."

I snorted, amused. "Do you want to hear about my night?"

"Oh, I need to tell you about mine first," Thistle said, digging into the nearest snowdrift. "So, do you remember the movie *Black X-Mas*?"

I barked out a laugh. "I knew it. She let something slip about your story when she was with us, and I knew you got *Black X-Mas*. Where were you? Was there a yellow guy in the walls?"

"Mrs. Little was in the walls," Thistle replied. "But I'm getting ahead of myself. So, we woke up in this sorority house and, I'm not joking, it was so pink it would've made a *My Pretty Pony* throw up.

"I knew we were in trouble right from the start, even though Marcus was convinced it was a dream," she continued. "I thought it was a punishment curse or something – I mean, what would I hate more than sorority girls, right? – but we were only there for, like, ten minutes, and then one of the girls had a knife sticking out of her eye."

"Nice." I joined in the shoveling. "How many people died?"

"Pretty much all of them. Like, twenty girls. We couldn't leave until we admitted we were terrible people and that Christmas with Aunt Tillie is better than Christmas in a sorority house. I don't care how angry I am at that woman, it wasn't hard to admit. Christmas with Aunt Tillie is better than a house full of dead sorority girls."

"What about live sorority girls?"

"Oh, it's definitely better than that," Thistle said. "What about you guys? What Christmas nightmare did you get?"

"*A Witchmas Carol.*"

"What?" Thistle furrowed her brow. "You mean from the Christmas book?"

"I nodded. We were visited by two ghosts and Aunt Tillie, and shown the past, present and future."

"Huh." Thistle's expression was hard to read. "How did that all work out?"

"Well, for starters, Aunt Tillie handled the past. She took us to the Christmas before we got Sugar … and then I got to see Sugar again."

Thistle brightened. "How'd he look?"

"Just as cute as I remembered."

Thistle smiled. "This summer we should go up to that spot where we buried him. We haven't been there in two years."

She was right. "We'll take some bacon."

"Don't mention bacon," Landon called out. He was making tremendous progress now that he had Marcus helping him. That was good news for me, because I was more interested in relating my evening to Thistle than in shoveling snow.

"I also got to see Landon as a little boy and teenager," I added. "He was very cute when he was little, but he was a total tool as a teenager."

"Oh, do tell."

"Don't tell," Landon groused.

"I kind of want to hear it, too," Marcus admitted.

"Well, for starters, his hair was even longer than it is now, and he drove a car shaped like a penis," I announced.

"That car was not shaped like a penis," Landon barked. "It was a Camaro. A Camaro is a classic car."

"Shaped like a penis," I added.

"It was not shaped like a penis!"

I waved off his feigned outrage. "He had a pretty blonde girlfriend named Shelly who was very dramatic. She cried because he was going to break up with her."

"What did he do?"

"Acted like a tool."

"That sounds about right." Thistle shot Landon a challenging look when he opened his mouth to protest. "Bay is telling the story. When it's your turn, I'll point at you."

"This family makes me tired," Landon complained, rolling his eyes.

"Then we spent some time in the present with Uncle Calvin as our guide," I said. "It was cool to hang out with him, but his stay was kind of boring. He basically made us watch Chief Terry and our mothers prepare for some charity dinner they have planned for this afternoon. Did you know they were doing that, by the way?"

"What charity dinner?"

I filled her in on everything I knew, and when I was finished she was as dumbfounded as me. "Why wouldn't they tell us about that?"

"I have no idea."

"They can't blame us for not knowing."

"I knew," Marcus offered, drawing three sets of eyes in his direction. "What? Everyone in town has been buzzing about it. We're busing people here from shelters in a number of towns so we can throw a huge party. They're attending the Christmas festival and everything."

How did I not know about that? My guilt doubled. "Well ... we'll have to make sure we donate time and whatever else they need."

"Yeah," Thistle agreed.

"We will, Bay," Landon said, pinning his eyes to mine. "We didn't know. We can still fix it. Don't freak out or anything."

"I'm not going to freak out." I wasn't. I might pout a bit, but I wasn't going to freak out.

"You're leaving out the best part of the story," Landon prodded. "Tell Thistle about what happened when we went to the future."

"Oh, right."

Thistle grinned, happy to have something to think about other than the fact that we were so self-absorbed we didn't realize we missed out on a big Hemlock Cove charity event. "I'm dying to hear what you saw in the future. How did I hold up?"

That was an interesting question. "Well ... you go back to a muted brown hair color at some point."

"That doesn't sound cool."

"You also have five children."

"Five?" Thistle's mouth dropped open. "There's no way I managed to keep my hips from spreading after giving birth to five children. That is outrageous."

"All boys."

"Boys?" Thistle looked horrified, but Marcus' face expressed interest.

"We had five boys? That sounds kind of fun. That's a basketball team."

"That does not sound fun," Thistle muttered.

"You didn't have five boys together," I added. "You had one boy together: Mace."

"Mace? Like Windu?" Thistle was on the verge of losing it. "Wait ... what do you mean we didn't have all of them together?"

"It's important you realize that Aunt Tillie was being vengeful," I cautioned. "Nothing we saw is going to really happen. The more I tell you, the more you'll come to realize that."

"Fine." Thistle heaved out a long-suffering sigh. "Lay it on me."

"Well, you had five boys with five different fathers."

"I'll kill that old witch!"

I ignored Thistle's outburst. "Let's see, you had Mace – the boy you shared with Marcus – and Fennel, oh, and Red Pepper Flake."

"Now you're just making stuff up!"

"That's what I said when I first heard the names," I admitted. "Your boys had the worst names by far. Landon and I were the parents of three teenagers – all girls – and apparently we named them Sage, Saffron and Sumac."

Thistle laughed so hard I thought she'd knock herself over. "Sumac?"

"Yeah. That's when I knew we were going to be fine looking around the future because it was so ridiculous. That was before we found out that the Earth now has two suns because the previous one exploded and two benevolent alien races tugged new suns into orbit for us."

"So you went to a future that Aunt Tillie dreamed up after watching a *Star Trek* marathon, huh?"

Now that she was hearing the details, Thistle wasn't as bothered. "Pretty much. You'll also be interested to know that Hemlock Cove had its own pope and king ... ."

"You were the king," Landon informed Marcus. "No joke. Apparently you took over when Aunt Tillie stepped down after she figured she'd ruled long enough."

"Well, that's kind of fun." Marcus smiled. "I was probably lonely without my Thistle, but being king is cool."

"You weren't lonely," I countered. "You had a second wife named Storm. She was suffering from PTSD and made porn films to get through it."

"I'm totally going to rip that old lady's head off," Thistle screeched. She was clearly back to being miffed.

"Who are we talking about?" Clove asked, appearing at the end of the driveway with Sam and two shovels in tow.

"Aunt Tillie," Thistle replied. "I'm going to kill her when I see her. Just prepare yourselves."

"Why?"

I gave Clove a brief rundown of my night, catching her up to where we were in the conversation. When I was done, she was bent over at the waist she laughed so hard.

"Fennel," she giggled, after the laugh storm subsided.

"I wouldn't talk," I said, hoping to take the edge off Thistle's anger. "You had a daughter named Cinnamon and spent all of your time in the corner staring at yourself in a mirror. I barely talked to you. Of course, that might have something to do with the fact that Aunt Tillie kept telling people I was one of the Upper Peninsula Winchesters."

Thistle and Clove shuddered in unison.

"I need to meet these other Winchesters," Landon said. "They sound fascinating."

"Then we're clearly telling the story wrong," Thistle fired back. "What do you think that was about? Clove sitting in the corner, I mean. It's obvious why she did what she did to me."

"Including making me king," Marcus added. "I'm obviously her favorite."

"No one likes a show-off," Landon muttered.

I ignored him. "Yeah. I have an idea about that, but we'll talk on the way to the inn. I think I've come up with something to fix Aunt Tillie's abandonment problem and punish her in the process."

"Oh, I'm already game for that," Thistle enthused, causing me to smile.

"Speaking of nights, what happened to you, Clove? I knew what Thistle was going through, but I had no idea what hoops Aunt Tillie asked you to jump through."

"Let's just say that doing *Rudolph the Red-Nosed Reindeer* – completely with Claymation – is no longer on my bucket list," Clove sneered. "Do you have any idea how hard it is to get clay out of certain cracks?"

And just like that, we had the Christmas spirit – and the driveway was clear to boot.

" Christmas isn't always about getting things. It's about giving things, too. That's the most important thing to remember. You need to give what you can and be gracious about what's given to you. Then, when you're done with that, you can smite your enemies with a clear conscience. Everyone clear? Okay, fasten your combat helmets and get ready. We're not done tonight until Margaret Little is in tears. Only then can we have our cookies.

— *A*unt Tillie while on babysitting duty on Christmas Eve

TWENTY

"Merry Christmas!"

Thistle bellowed the words as we stomped in through the front door of The Overlook. The snow wiped out the pathway between the guesthouse and inn, so we had no choice but to drive and park in the front lot.

Mom was behind the counter when we entered. Her eyes widened when she saw all six of us. "What are you doing here?"

"It's Christmas," I replied. "Where else would we be on Christmas?"

"Nowhere else," Landon answered for me, sliding behind the counter to give Mom a kiss on the cheek. "We all decided this was the place to be for Christmas."

Mom didn't bother to hide her awe. "But ... how? You were all so sure last night."

"Yes, and then we spent some hard hours searching our souls," Thistle replied, her eyes dark when she moved them to the open doorway between the lobby and the kitchen. "Merry Christmas, Aunt Tillie."

"Merry Christmas, mouth." Aunt Tillie was one big smile when she stepped into the room. She looked a little too pleased with herself. "Merry Christmas to all of you."

Mom, as if sensing the chill in the room, shifted from one foot to the other. "Is something going on?"

"I don't know," I replied. "Is something going on, Aunt Tillie?"

"It's Christmas and we had a blizzard last night," Aunt Tillie replied, her face reflecting innocence. "What else could possibly be going on?"

Mom wasn't convinced, but she didn't press the issue. "Well, the good news is that you're here just in time to see Annie open her gifts. I heard Belinda upstairs trying to corral her a few minutes ago. She's very excited to see if Santa brought her anything."

"We dropped off our gifts yesterday, so she should have quite the haul," Thistle noted. "I'm glad we didn't miss it."

"I am, too." Mom patted Landon's hand. "Although, we kind of have plans for this afternoon."

"We know," I said smoothly. "We're going to the town party, too."

"You are?"

"You didn't think you could get away with throwing a party without us, did you?" Clove asked, shrugging out of her coat. "We're looking forward to a party."

"Definitely," Landon agreed. "I love the shindigs Hemlock Cove throws. Will there be a kissing booth?" He'd been obsessed with the idea of the reoccurring kissing booth since the first time he saw it not long after we began dating.

"I already told you, it's called the mistletoe booth around Christmas," I supplied. "It's the same theme, except they hang mistletoe inside and you're allowed to drink hot chocolate while kissing."

"Sold." Landon grinned as he moved closer to me. "I think I've found my afternoon activity."

"And here I thought it would be making bacon angels or something," Mom teased, her eyes lighting with mischief.

"Yeah, well, I'm thinking about going on a diet." Landon patted his flat stomach.

I shot him a hard look. "Not on Christmas you're not."

"Right after the holidays then."

"Or maybe we'll start working out more," I suggested.

"Don't be a dirty pervert," Aunt Tillie chided, causing me to scold her with a look. "It's Christmas. You can't be a dirty pervert on Christmas."

"That shows what you know," Landon fired back. "I can be a dirty pervert any day of the year." He linked his fingers with mine and turned his eyes to the stairs when the sound of feet pounding from the third floor to the first caught his attention. "It sounds like someone is ready to see what Santa brought her."

I smiled when Annie appeared at the bottom of the stairs. Her hair was tousled from sleep, although it looked as if Belinda at least tried to run a brush through it. And she still wore her bright red pajamas. She pulled up short when she saw us, her eyes filling with wonder.

"Why are you here?"

"We're your Christmas presents," Marcus answered, smiling. "Merry Christmas, little one."

Annie, who adored Marcus under most circumstances, made an exaggerated face. "I already have you guys. Where are my real gifts?"

Thistle chuckled and pointed toward the dining room. "I think you should probably head in that direction."

Annie needed no further prodding, racing away from us and toward the room where her Christmas gifts awaited.

"I'm sorry about that," Belinda offered lamely. "She's just so … excited."

"There's no reason to apologize," Landon said. "We're all excited, too."

"And she might not realize it yet, but these six are part of her Christmas gift," Aunt Tillie added. The look on her face promised a full day of superiority. That was going to be hard to deal with. "They're certainly part of my Christmas gift, too."

Oh, well. Even Aunt Tillie could be sweet when she wanted to be.

Annie let loose with what strangely sounded like a war cry in the next room and we picked up our pace to join her. The mountain of gifts under the tree was staggering.

"Are all these for Annie?" I didn't begrudge the child her gifts –

she'd had a rough few years, after all – but the stack was almost dumbfounding.

"They're for everyone," Aunt Tillie replied. "Some of them are for Annie. I think, if you look carefully, some of them are for you."

All the resentment I'd been holding up to use against Aunt Tillie faded. "I'll bet there's something under there for you, too, right?"

"There's a lot of somethings under there for me," Aunt Tillie replied. "I also bought myself a new snowmobile. It's got tons of action under the hood and runs whisper silent so I'll be able to stalk Margaret Little good and proper."

"At least you have your priorities straight." I accepted the mug of hot chocolate Twila handed me as she entered the room and then settled in a chair next to Landon to watch Annie tear through her gifts. There would be plenty of time for the adults to open gifts when she was done. "Maybe, if you're really good, we'll go with you to mess with Mrs. Little before the town party."

I didn't know I was going to make the offer until it was already out of my mouth. Once I said the words, though, I felt better.

"We should definitely do that," Thistle enthused, perking up. "I think I can even remember how to make yellow snow."

"What's yellow snow?" Annie asked, grinning as she unwrapped a new doll. "Thank you, Marcus!"

Marcus beamed back at her. "You're welcome. That's the one you wanted, right?"

"Yes. I love her."

Landon lightly rubbed my back as he smiled indulgently at the girl. "Yellow snow is something that you never want to eat, Annie."

"Because it's old?"

"Because it's been peed on," Aunt Tillie answered, earning a hiss from Mom. "What? Why are you pointing at Belinda? I'm sure Belinda knows where yellow snow comes from. As for you all joining, I'm not sure you're worthy. I'll have to give it some thought."

"Something tells me we'll make the cut," Landon said, rubbing his cheek against mine as he rested his chin on my shoulder. "When are you going to spring your surprise on her?" He kept his voice low so Aunt Tillie couldn't hear over Annie's enthusiastic paper shredding.

"Soon. Not until Annie is done opening her gifts."

"Make sure I'm around when you tell her."

"You know I will."

We lapsed into amiable silence, comfortably sipping our hot chocolate while Annie let loose with a series of delighted shrieks and giggles. She was even excited by the new clothes Santa brought her – something that would've dragged down my spirits when I was her age. Clothes are simply unacceptable as a gift when you're younger than twelve. What? I didn't make it up. Aunt Tillie did, and it's one of the few things I agree with her on.

"Ho, ho, ho!"

I heard Chief Terry's booming voice in the other room and turned my head in that direction. I heard him banging his boots on the front rug and I excused myself to greet him. As if sensing I needed some alone time with him, Landon remained where he was.

"I'll keep your seat warm."

"I won't be gone long."

I found Chief Terry sitting on the front bench as he struggled to wrestle his boots off. He arched an eyebrow when he saw me approaching. "I thought you were spending the day alone with Landon."

"I had a change of heart."

"Really? Why?"

"Because Christmas should be spent with family," I replied. "Landon is a part of my family, but he's not the whole of it." I sat down next to Chief Terry. "You're part of my family, too."

Chief Terry isn't good at hiding his emotions. If he played poker he'd be much poorer because he's incapable of bluffing. "You're part of my family, too, sweetheart."

I leaned in and gave him a kiss on the cheek. That was only part of what I wanted to tell him. "So, last night Aunt Tillie punished us by putting us in her versions of Christmas stories. Thistle got *Black X-Mas*. Clove got *Rudolph The Red-Nosed Reindeer* – and I guess it was even more terrifying than *Black X-Mas* because of all the Claymation. And I got *A Witchmas Carol*."

"What's *A Witchmas Carol*?"

"*A Christmas Carol* for witches."

"I should've seen that coming. Continue."

"Most of what happened isn't important," I explained. "Basically Aunt Tillie wanted us to admit she was right and we were wrong and then promise to never spend another Christmas away from the family. We decided that early, but she punished us all the same."

"That sounds just like her."

"Landon and I went to the past and to the present, and then we landed in the future. We saw you setting up for the big party. I'm kind of angry that you didn't mention that to me, but we'll get to it later."

Chief Terry was obviously confused. "Was I in the future?"

"You were."

"What was I doing?"

"Eating."

"Okay ... well ... ."

"There was a message there about you, and I think Aunt Tillie just added it in with the other stuff because she wanted me to come to a realization," I explained. "Everything that happened in the future was a mess. It was her mess. She made Marcus a king and gave Hemlock Cove a pope."

"That sounds really odd."

"You have no idea," I said. "She also gave us all kids with terrible names, like Sumac, Cinnamon and Fennel."

Chief Terry chuckled, his broad shoulders shaking. "That sounds ... horrible."

"It wasn't horrible," I clarified. "It wasn't nice, mind you, but it wasn't horrible. I was happy to see you, but you were really fat."

"She made me fat?" Chief Terry's smile slipped. "What did I ever do to her?"

"It's not about that. You see, she wanted me to understand that maybe I've been holding you back."

Chief Terry stilled. "What do you mean by that?"

"Did I ever tell you I wanted you to marry my mother when I was younger?" I asked, changing tactics.

"No, but I think that's probably a common dream for kids."

"I did. I had that dream for a long time. Then I didn't."

"Why did you change your mind?"

"Because I was afraid that if I told you to make a decision – to pick between Mom, Marnie and Twila – that you'd pick Marnie or Twila, and then you'd like Clove or Thistle better than me."

"Sweetheart, that was never going to happen."

"I know that now, but ... I was a kid. Kids think stupid things."

"They do indeed."

"In the future, you were still trapped between the three of them and they would not stop feeding you. I thought you might explode at one point. That was before Landon stole your turkey leg."

"I have no idea what that means, and I'm not sure I want to."

"It really doesn't matter," I said, waving away the visual. "The thing is, I want you to know that it's okay to choose. I want you to be happy. You'll always be my surrogate father whether or not you choose Mom, Marnie or Twila.

"And, before you ask the obvious question, I know you might choose none of them," I continued. "I'm okay with that, too. I only want you to be happy."

"What makes you think I'm not happy?"

"I don't know that you're not. I simply want to make sure that you are. I want you to have someone – like I have Landon – and I don't want you to be forced to eat three different versions of pie every meal for the rest of your life. It's not healthy."

Chief Terry chuckled as he slung an arm around my shoulders, seemingly amused by my plight. "Well, I don't need your permission, but I thank you for it all the same."

"I'm not saying you need to do anything about it now," I clarified. "I want you to give it some thought. Think about it as a Christmas gift for me."

Chief Terry's eyes were somber when they met mine. "Then I will give it some thought."

We sat like that for a moment, staring at each other, and then Aunt Tillie burst into the room. The look she shot us was one full of pure annoyance.

"Why are you in here?"

"We had a few things to talk about," I replied, agitation bubbling up. Now I remembered exactly why I was angry with her.

"You didn't tell him about the yellow snow plan, did you?"

"Oh, geez." Chief Terry pressed his eyes shut. "I don't want to know what evil plan you've cooked up for Margaret Little. It's Christmas. I'm off the clock."

"That's good to know." Aunt Tillie's smile was serene. "I might allow you and your cousins to join me for a brief trip this afternoon if you're good. I haven't come to a firm decision, though."

"Oh, that's too bad," I drawled. "We've come to a firm decision after discussing what happened last night."

"Nothing happened." Aunt Tillie shot me a quelling look. "Why do you think something happened?"

"I already told Chief Terry, so there's no point in lying," I said. "Thistle, Clove and I had a long discussion about what the dreams meant."

"We did," Thistle confirmed, her eyes filled with malice as she drifted into the room with Clove and Landon on her heels. Clove was as angry as Thistle, but Landon simply wanted to see the show. "We had a very long talk about what your actions really signified."

Aunt Tillie did her best to remain calm, but I didn't miss her hard swallow. "And what did you decide?"

"We decided that you're acting out because you're lonely," Clove replied. "We never wanted that for you, so we're going to fix it."

"That's right," I added. "We're going to make sure that you have a special lunch every week with all three of us, a time when we can catch up and make sure you're not lonely."

"We're having it Thursday afternoons," Thistle said. "We're really looking forward to it."

Aunt Tillie balked. "Thursday afternoons? That's when I spy on those idiots at the senior center."

"Oh, you'll be far too busy for stuff like that," I said. "We're also going to come up with a schedule to make sure you're covered throughout the week. We thought – since you're obviously lonely without us – that you could spend time at the store and the newspaper office."

"We want to keep an eye on you," Thistle said. "You're our great-aunt. You deserve our undivided attention."

Aunt Tillie narrowed her eyes, frustration positively rolling off her. "Okay. You've made your point. I get it."

"Oh, we're not even close to making our point," I countered. "We think it will take weeks for it to sink in. The most important thing to us is making sure you feel safe and comfortable. It's clear that you're not feeling either."

Chief Terry and Landon laughed as Aunt Tillie's face flooded with color.

"That sounds like a fabulous idea," Chief Terry offered. "I think that extra time with your great-nieces can only make things better. Now, in the spring, you won't have to waste time gardening by yourself."

"That is a great idea," Landon enthused.

Aunt Tillie extended a finger, pointing it at all of us in turn. "I know exactly what you're doing. It won't work."

"We're not doing anything but loving you," Clove cooed.

"Ugh. You're all on my list!"

Printed in Great Britain
by Amazon